# The Lovegrove Hermit

*By the same author*

The Secret House
The Abbey Governess
Templewood
The Dark City
Surgeons' Square
The Crooked Street
Devil's Folly

# The Lovegrove Hermit

## Rosemary Craddock

ROBERT HALE · LONDON

ISBN 978-0-7198-1106-7

Robert Hale Limited
Clerkenwell House
Clerkenwell Green
London EC1R 0HT

www.halebooks.com

2 4 6 8 10 9 7 5 3 1

Typeset in New Century Schoolbook
Printed in the UK by the Berforts Group

# CHAPTER ONE

On the seventh anniversary of Harry's death I took his amethyst ring from my left hand and transferred it to the right. I had no hope of loving anyone as I had loved Harry O'Neill but it was now in the past and far away in time and place. My prospects of happiness were buried with Harry's mangled body at Badajos.

I had made a life for myself of sorts – pleasant enough in its way but utterly lacking in the highs and lows of youth. I was now twenty-nine and for some years I had lived with my brother George at Fairfield in Gloucestershire, acting as companion-governess to my niece Sophie. My father was a poor clergyman but whereas the younger boys had been obliged to make their own way in the army, navy, and church, my eldest brother, George, had been adopted by our childless uncle who had made him heir to his estate. He had succeeded to the property about the time his wife died and I came to live at the manor house.

George had shown no inclination to remarry so I was treated as mistress of the house. It was quite an enviable position, I suppose, but I was always conscious of the fact that I would be ousted if my brother did eventually stir himself sufficiently to find another wife.

I must not be too critical of George, who was the kindest of men. Like all of us, he had failings but they were of the gentler sort. He was, perhaps, too easy-going and inclined to take the path of least resistance. No greater contrast could be imagined to my beloved Harry – active, energetic, reckless, impulsive, and wildly ambitious. I never laughed so much as when I was with him or suffered so much when we were parted.

I still kept by my bed a small watercolour portrait of him which I had painted myself, but I had never been quite satisfied with it because the essential spark of life was missing. However, I had caught the tilt of his head with its tousled dark curls and a hint of that alert expression and, of course, the dashing green uniform of the Rifles.

That was all I had of him: his ring, a lock of his hair, a few letters and my amateurish portrait. There were also memories, too painful in the beginning, and now fading like dreams.

That summer of 1819 was glorious. One languid afternoon in June, as Sophie and I were walking through the grounds of Fairfield we saw George reclining under a tree, his back against the trunk and his legs stretched out before him on the grass. He waved a sheet of paper in the air and beckoned us to join him.

'How do you fancy a trip to Derbyshire?' he smiled. 'We are invited to stay at Lovegrove Priory.'

'A priory?' cried Sophie, 'how romantic! Who lives there?'

'That second cousin of ours who writes those Gothicky novels you like so much.'

'Mrs Webb,' I said, 'although they are published anonymously.'

'By "a Lady",' added Sophie. 'I've read them all – *An Italian Romance*, *The Castle of Rodolfo*, *Leonora and Rodrigo*. . . .'

'I tried reading one once,' sighed George, 'but gave up at the third chapter. Not my sort of thing at all.'

'But why has she suddenly asked us? We've never had much to do with her.' I was decidedly puzzled by the unexpected invitation. An occasional letter was exchanged but that was all. I always had to write a reply to her effusive missives because George said he was no use at letter-writing unless it was on business. I believe she used to visit our uncle and aunt at Fairfield many years ago before she was married. George remembered vaguely though he was a boy of twelve at the time.

'A rather overwhelming lady, I seem to recall. She can't have been more than eighteen at the time but she seemed much older. She was travelling with some female dragon companion. I do remember her hugging me and calling me a dear little fellow.' He shuddered at the recollection.

'No harm in her, I suppose,' he continued. 'Anyway, she married a Mr Webb, who carried her off to the North and then died leaving her with a son. Then she married again a few years ago – a Sir Ralph Denby.'

'I remember she wrote and told us,' I added, 'and later we had a letter from Italy telling us about their travels.'

'And the baronet lives at the Priory?' enquired Sophie.

'Not when he first married Cousin Amelia. And he's not a baronet, merely a knight on account of serving as mayor and helping the local MP get elected. He made a fortune in cotton mills and then sold up, married Amelia and started looking for a country estate. He settled on a fine old Tudor house called Lovegrove Priory. He'd been married before too and has a daughter about your age, Sophie, so if we go there she'd be a friend for you.'

'When can we go?' cried Sophie, who was not much interested in the possibility of friendship with an unknown girl but excited by the prospect of staying in an ancient house with Gothic ruins.

'She suggests the 22nd as she has one or two other friends staying there at that time. Here – read her letter.'

He handed it to me and Sophie and I read it together. It was in her usual exaggerated style, professing a great desire to renew acquaintance with dear George and his dear sister and dear little Sophie whom she was *dying* to see. Sir Ralph was also eager to meet us and we could be sure of a hearty welcome to the ancient halls of Lovegrove.

I wondered again why Amelia Denby had invited us to stay. It was not until we arrived at Lovegrove that I understood.

# CHAPTER TWO

We travelled to Lovegrove swiftly and in considerable comfort as George had hired a post-chaise and four. The first night we broke our journey at Leamington and arrived next day at Lovegrove in the warm light of late afternoon. On driving through the well-wooded park, we saw the priory ruins ahead of us and beyond them the house, a long, low building of mellow stone, the sun twinkling on its windows. At least, George and I saw the house. Sophie, who was sitting opposite and consequently looking backwards, gave a sudden gasp.

'Is it romantic enough for you?' her father enquired.

'What?' She looked startled.

'The house.'

'Is it haunted?'

George laughed. 'I don't know – you'll have to ask the Denbys.'

'But I saw something – someone – back there by those trees. Then he was gone.'

George and I both craned back to see the place she had indicated and saw no one.

'What did you see?' I asked.

'A tall man in a long grey robe with a hood. I think he had a beard.'

'I doubt if he was a ghost,' said George, somewhat amused. 'Probably a woodcutter in a smock. I shouldn't think a self-respecting ghost would appear at this time of day. Don't they wait for moonlight and owls and so forth?'

'It wasn't a man in a smock. It was a monk.'

'You've read too many novels,' said George. 'Can't you wean her off them?' he asked me, but his tone remained jocular.

Sophie flushed and took on a stubborn look I knew well. At seventeen she was not immune to the swiftly changing moods of extreme youth but she had a happy, sunny nature that made people warm to her. She had no great depth of intellect but was bright and quick as well as extremely pretty. When she saw the house, she forgot her annoyance and exclaimed with delight at its beauty and antiquity.

The family were waiting to greet us. A very tall, statuesque lady in a turban with many flowing shawls and scarves held out her arms in an extravagant gesture of welcome. She embraced us all enthusiastically.

'My dear! How delightful to see you!' She wasted no more time on me after a quick peck on the cheek.

'Why, Cousin George!' she cried. 'You've grown so tall we are now of a height!'

That made her five feet ten if an inch.

'If I'd stayed the same height as when you saw me last I'd now be in a circus,' he smiled.

'And so handsome!' She pinched his check roguishly and he winced but she was quite oblivious to his embarrassment. George *was* handsome but less so than when he was in his twenties. At forty-two, indolence and a hearty appetite had filled out his face and blurred what was once an elegant figure. A sweet smile and a benign expression were some compensation.

'Ah, the poor motherless child!' Lady Denby descended on the unfortunate Sophie. 'My dear, dear girl! You must look on me as your mother while you are here.'

Sophie cast a helpless look in my direction before she was once more pressed to her ladyship's ample bosom.

'I thought I was being suffocated,' she told me afterwards, 'and that horrid scent she uses makes it worse.'

'You'll have to put up with it, I'm afraid. At least she doesn't seem disposed to embrace me like that.'

It was later I noticed Lady Denby called George and Sophie 'cousin' but I was always 'Miss Tyler'.

Amelia Denby, despite her overwhelming presence, seemed good-natured and cheerful, with a hearty laugh, though I was to discover she had little sense of humour. She obviously enjoyed being admired and her most devoted adulator was her husband, Sir Ralph Denby. He was half a head shorter than his wife, portly, balding, red-faced and seemingly devoted to his spouse, whom he regarded as a goddess beyond reproach.

She was indeed a handsome woman with rather heavy classical features like a statue of Juno. A number of glossy, raven-black ringlets escaped from her turban and I recollected George had described her as 'fairish' which I interpreted as light brown like my brother and me. I supposed she wore a wig to disguise any greyness and because she thought black hair more suited to a writer of romantic novels.

A rather plain, sandy-haired girl who had been hanging back behind her elders was now brought forward and introduced as Sir Ralph's daughter, Elinor – the progeny of his first wife. This was the young woman whom Lady Denby had suggested might make a nice friend for Sophie – who seemed unimpressed.

The girl was certainly no great beauty but I thought she could have done more with her appearance. She had a good figure, fine hazel eyes, nondescript features and a disastrous hairstyle, all scraped back from a slightly bulging forehead. She was very plainly attired in an unflattering greyish-brown dress with no adornments save a mud-coloured sash. She shrank into the background as quickly as she could and Sophie never spared her a second glance.

'Our little party is not yet complete,' said Sir Ralph. 'My wife's son is due here tomorrow. So are Mrs Thorpe and her nephew.'

'An old schoolfellow of mine,' explained Lady Denby. 'We have been friends since we were girls. I haven't yet met her nephew. Now, do follow me and I'll show you to your rooms. Usually we dine at five but it will be six tonight to give you a chance to recover from your journey.'

She led us through the porch into an oak-panelled entrance hall from which a magnificent carved staircase rose to the floor above. It was lit by a large stained-glass window full of heraldic splendour which had nothing to do with either Sir Ralph or his wife.

'The house was built largely of masonry from the Old Priory,' Lady Denby explained as she conducted us upstairs. 'You will have seen the ruins near the house. The land was originally purchased by Sir William Chater after the

Dissolution of the Monasteries. He had this house built and although there have been some modern alterations and additions, the building is much the same as in Tudor times. The Chater family were great supporters of Henry VIII but after the death of Edward VI they made the mistake of offering allegiance to Lady Jane Grey.'

'I hope you are absorbing all this history,' I whispered to Sophie, who was clattering up the uncarpeted steps with a look of fierce concentration.

'Sir William was executed and his property confiscated,' Lady Denby continued, her voice booming out above us, 'and after that it fell into the hands of a Catholic family who supported Queen Mary. They hung onto it through all the years of persecution – I must show you our priest-hole tomorrow.'

'A priest-hole!' cried Sophie delightedly. 'Are there secret passages too?'

'None that I know of, my dear, though there are legends of such. The Catholic Langleys grew poorer until they were forced to sell their property to the Wiltons, who lived here for more than a hundred years before dying out. That's when Sir Ralph acquired the estate and spent a great deal of time and money restoring the house before bringing me here. There is so much to show you but we'll leave that until tomorrow when you are rested.'

My room was next to Sophie on the first floor. After seeing us safely installed our hostess departed, saying she would see us in the Great Hall before dinner. Our maid Betsey was busy unpacking our luggage and moving from one room to another.

'Where's Papa?' asked Sophie, putting her head round my door.

'I haven't the faintest idea,' I replied. 'He's at the other end of the passage, I think. Do you like your room?'

'Oh, yes – very historical and romantic. I see we both have the same view of the park. It's a pity we're at the back so we can't see the priory ruins.'

'No, but we have a lovely view of the lake.'

'Your room is considerably smaller than mine,' she said. 'You ought to have had the larger. Would you like to change over?'

'No, this will do very well and I'm sure Lady Denby planned our accommodation quite deliberately.'

'I didn't think much of Elinor Denby,' she said, changing the subject abruptly. 'A very plain creature!'

'Very clever, I believe.'

'A bluestocking!' Sophie sniffed. 'I don't see why anyone should suppose I'd want to be friends with her.'

'You don't know her yet.'

'I'm not sure I want to. I wonder what the son, Rowland, is like.'

'I'm sure we'll find out all too soon.'


That evening in the gloomy, dark-panelled dining-room Lady Denby – now adorned with an even more splendid turban of crimson silk with gold fringes – mentioned her son Rowland at regular intervals. He was apparently a paragon of all the virtues and a great favourite with everyone on account of his winning ways.

'Do you happen to have any ghosts here?' asked George, who was obviously keen to hear of something else. 'Most old houses seem to have a White Lady, or a headless Cavalier.'

'Well, there are legends, I must admit,' said Sir Ralph,

'though I've never seen or heard anything myself.'

'You have not the necessary temperament, my dear,' said his wife, not unkindly. 'You have spent so many years as a practical man of business that the ability to sense the other world is quite stifled. Now *I*, whose imagination is fully developed, have detected certain supernatural phenomena: cold spots, footsteps when no one is there, doors opening and closing without human contact.'

'But you haven't actually *seen* anything?' said George.

'Not yet,' she conceded, rather reluctantly. 'But people claim to have heard chanting in the ruins of the old priory church and in the house the Tapestry Room is supposed to be haunted. It's one of the bedrooms but never used. In the past, people have seen the grey phantom of a lady in Tudor dress, moaning and sighing for her husband, Sir William Chater, who was taken off to the Tower.'

'And shortened by a head, I suppose,' added George facetiously. 'There isn't the ghost of a monk, by any chance? Sophie thought she saw one this afternoon as we were coming up the drive.'

'Papa!' Sophie looked highly embarrassed.

No one laughed, fortunately, though I saw a faint smile on Elinor Denby's face.

'A tall fellow in a grey hooded robe?' enquired Sir Ralph.

'Yes.'

'Oh, you're not the first visitor he's startled. But he's not a ghost; he's our hermit.'

'A hermit?' cried Sophie. 'Then I didn't imagine him?'

'Of course not,' said Lady Denby, 'he's Brother Caspar. I insisted we should acquire a hermit when we came to live here and Sir Ralph had a very comfortable cave constructed for him before we advertised.'

'A comfortable cave seems a bit of a contradiction,' said George.

'Oh, it has perfectly adequate living accommodation at the back, out of sight,' Sir Ralph explained. 'We send food down from the house and he has a little fireplace where he can boil a kettle and so forth.'

'What sort of man would choose to live as a hermit?' I wondered. 'I suppose he had to be someone unsociable. An old vagrant perhaps, grateful for food and shelter.'

'Not at all,' said Lady Denby, 'he's quite an educated man and not all that ancient. He simply wants to live apart from the world – a misanthrope. But he's so picturesque he adds the final touch of mystery and romance to our park.'

After dinner, we ladies retired to the drawing room, which was a good deal brighter and more cheerful than the rest of the house as it had been altered in the last century. It was comfortably furnished and contained modern pictures and ornaments. There were large sash windows and the walls were painted pale green.

'Not at all in keeping with the rest of the house, I'm afraid,' said Lady Denby. 'Sir Ralph and I plan to restore the casement windows. Now I really must lie down, I've had such an exhausting day.' She reclined on a sofa propped up with cushions and allowed Elinor to dispense the tea and coffee.

I found that Amelia Denby, when not actually engaged in novel-writing, spent much of her time on a sofa, sometimes reading but often deep in slumber.

'I am afraid my devotion to my muse drains my energy and I must rest frequently as I am not robust by nature but cursed with a delicate constitution.'

I darted a warning glance at Sophie, who was in danger of giggling. Lady Denby asked if she played the piano.

'A little,' said Sophie, who managed to control her mirth, 'but I suppose that's what all young ladies say.'

'Then you must entertain us, my dear, but before you start, do take a look at that portrait of my son near the piano. I've had candles put near it so it's well illuminated.'

I joined Sophie in front of the painting. It was a half-length of a fair-haired young man in a blue coat. Either the artist had flattered him or he really was strikingly handsome with his mother's Grecian features and a debonair attitude.

'He looks very nice,' said Sophie cautiously.

'Wait till you see him in the flesh,' simpered Lady Denby. 'He's so charming, It's such a pity he can't be here more often but he has so many friends and is engaged in so many activities.'

'What does he do?' asked Sophie.

'*Do*? What should he do?'

'I mean, is he in any profession – the law, perhaps, or the Church or the army or – or – something,' she ended lamely.

'There is no need for him to *work*. He is of independent means.'

Anyone would think, I pondered, that her ladyship had not married a man who had made a fortune in industry and whose father had worked in a mill.

Sophie played for us – rather well for her.

'Such a pretty girl!' pronounced Lady Denby. 'Her hair is a true gold – just like Rowland's!'

When Sir Ralph and George joined us, Elinor Denby was prevailed upon to play and displayed a talent quite outstanding.

'Good, isn't she?' said Sir Ralph proudly.

'Yes indeed,' I agreed, 'quite superb. She must have been well taught – but even that cannot create real talent.'

Having reached the end of the piece, Elinor put away her music and retired to a corner of the room with her embroidery. I went over to her.

'Miss Denby, I have rarely heard an amateur pianist play so well.'

'Thank you. Not many people appreciate my efforts.'

'I find that hard to believe.'

'But few people ever hear me and those who do know little about music. Besides, I am outshone in every department by the wondrous Rowland.'

'Surely he doesn't play.'

'Of course not – he doesn't do anything except waste time and money.'

She sounded bitter and I realized how difficult it must be for her – the only child of an amiable and loving father – forced to share a house with his domineering second wife and at times with her obviously spoilt son.

'I can hardly wait to meet him,' I said drily and she smiled in sympathy.

Later at bedtime, Sophie came into my room while I was brushing my hair.

'I'm tired out,' she said 'and it isn't just the journey. I find Lady Denby quite exhausting. It's difficult to believe she wrote those wonderful books.'

'Have you told her how much you admire them?'

'Oh yes.'

'Hmm – I'm not sure you should have done that. Don't let

her like you too much, Sophie, I'm afraid she has plans for you.'

'What sort of plans?'

'Well, you remember how we all wondered why she asked us here. She has a marriageable son of twenty-three. You are an heiress and very eligible.'

Sophie was aghast. 'But I may not like him – or he may not like me.'

'One can only hope. . . .' I said.

# CHAPTER THREE

The next morning after breakfast, our hosts took us on a tour of the house. It was one of those sprawling, half-planned dwellings that seemed quite confusing at first. I found much of it rather dark and gloomy with a minstrels' gallery and all manner of little parlours and long corridors, faded tapestries, odd steps going up and down, creaking doors and ancient carved panelling. It was crammed with ancient artefacts collected by Sir Ralph: suits of armour and fearsome weapons of war – halberds and battleaxes, swords and maces.

We were vouchsafed a glimpse of Lady Denby's study which opened out of the library. It looked as though a gale had blown through as it was littered with papers and piles of books. A large, rather masculine desk stood in the middle of the room. It was there, we were told in hushed tones, she wrote her novels.

Sophie was eager to see the Priest's Hole which was concealed inside a cupboard built into the panelling of a bedroom. A trap door in the floor revealed a ladder leading down to a tiny enclosure where there was no room for anyone above middle height to stand upright. Sophie insisted on going down but found it 'full of spiders' and hastily scrambled out again.

'There's supposed to be another somewhere but no one's ever found it,' said Sir Ralph.

He then lead us up to the Long Gallery, which was a handsome room running the length of the house, with windows down one side so it was well lit. It had been transformed by Sir Ralph into a repository for his collection. This was an extraordinary conglomeration of objects. I caught sight of an Egyptian mummy case – without an occupant, to Sophie's dismay – the skeleton of a crocodile and a cabinet full of mineral specimens.

Sir Ralph explained that there was really not enough time this morning to show us the collection properly.

'Let's wait for a wet day and then we can really look at everything in detail,' he said. 'We'll take advantage of the fine weather by a little tour of the park. Are you up to it, my dear?' he asked his wife, who looked thoughtful.

'If we don't go too far,' she said. 'If I begin to flag I shall return to the house and leave the walk to you. I'm sure you won't mind?' She turned to George and me and we assured her we wouldn't mind at all. Sir Ralph seemed a very pleasant man, and he was certainly easier company than his wife. Lady Denby did manage to accompany us for the first half-hour.

'We'll go by the hermitage,' she said, 'as you seem so interested. The hermit may not be there, of course, because he does wander about. He is not allowed to leave the park or to talk to anyone unless absolutely necessary.'

'How awful!' cried Sophie.

'It's his own choice. He gets his keep and ten guineas a year. He can leave if he doesn't like it, though it would be difficult to find anyone as perfect to fill his place.'

We reached the end of a winding path overshadowed by trees and came to a rocky outcrop. How much was natural and how much contrived by man it was difficult to tell, but there was the cave and there, in the entrance, sat the hermit, reading a book.

'Good morrow, Brother Caspar!' cried Lady Denby and Sophie snatched out her handkerchief and covered her mouth. I could see her shoulders shaking; George's lips twitched.

The hermit rose to his feet and bowed his head, his hands folded over his book.

'May I speak to him?' I asked, anxious to detract attention away from Sophie.

'Well, yes,' said Lady Denby rather reluctantly, 'though we don't encourage it. You may get a strange reply.'

'What are you reading, Brother Caspar?' I enquired.

'Words – words – words.' The voice was deep and cultivated; the face, behind its greying beard, gaunt and rather handsome, but with an expression of deep melancholy.

'I told you so!' exclaimed our hostess and I wondered if she knew he was quoting *Hamlet*.

I found myself wanting to know more about him. Who was he? What had happened in his life to bring him here, forsaking human companionship and the comforts that make life pleasant?

Amelia Denby drew her hand across her brow. 'I'm growing weary,' she said. 'I'm afraid I must go back to the house. My Muse calls me. I find if I let a single day go by without writing it takes an immense effort to start again. I'm sure you won't mind if Sir Ralph finishes the walk with you. Be sure you see the little temple by the lake and the priory ruins in front of the house. I will see you at luncheon.'

Then she was gone and the atmosphere lightened. The hermit returned to his book and we resumed our walk.

'She must write every day or she becomes quite ill,' explained Sir Ralph. 'You must excuse the effects of the artistic temperament. She is very delicate.'

I glared at Sophie, who was on the verge of giggling again. Poor Sir Ralph was obviously devoted to his overbearing wife, whom he struggled to understand.

That afternoon George went out with Sir Ralph for a ride round the estate. Lady Denby had not appeared at luncheon but sent her apologies. She was 'taking a bite' in her study while working on her latest novel which was provisionally entitled 'The Spanish Bandit'.

After the meal she sent Elinor to us to take us up on the roof to look at the view.

'My stepmama is too immersed in her writing to delight us with her company,' she said. 'I'm sure she'll be sorely missed.' There was a distinct note of irony in her voice. 'I have brought along papa's old telescope, which adds enchantment to the view – "where every prospect pleases—"'

'"And only man is vile",' added Sophie. Elinor looked at her in surprise.

We followed Miss Denby up to the attics and then ascended a twisting timber stair to a small door which opened onto the leads. At once we found ourselves surrounded by a forest of chimneys, most of them highly decorated, and I was pleased to see a sturdy, castellated parapet on the edge of the roof. I can tolerate heights well enough if protected by an adequate barrier between the drop and me.

Elinor handed me the telescope and I leaned my elbows on a stone crenellation and focused on the park behind the house. It was a beautiful, peaceful view with nothing to disturb the tranquillity save a gardener with his wheelbarrow. I could see the lake, the walls of the kitchen garden and the top of the rocky outcrop above the hermitage. I could even see the chimney which was invisible from the ground. Beyond the park were fields and blue-green wooded hills in a heat haze. I passed the telescope to Sophie and found Elinor watching me curiously.

'You are not at all what I expected,' she said.

'Why, what did you expect?'

'Someone older and more auntish, I suppose. Certainly no one pretty and elegant.'

'Thank you. I'm sure if I ever become 'auntish' Sophie will tell me.'

We wandered about for a while and then I took the telescope to look over the grounds at the front of the house. The only picturesque elements were the ruined priory and the distant arched gate at the end of the drive. At first the scene seemed as uneventful as that at the rear but then a figure caught my eye. It was the hermit, quite near the clump of trees where Sophie had seen him the previous day. Then I saw a horseman riding down the driveway. He dismounted and walked towards the hermit, handed him a package and stood for a few minutes, deep in conversation.

'What can you see?' asked Sophie, peering in the direction of the telescope. 'I can't quite make it out – there's a horse—'

'It's not my stepbrother, is it?' asked Elinor.

To me it looked like a man in a blue coat and a grey hat

– a gentleman, I felt sure, judging by the handsome horse. There was something odd about his appearance but I could not determine what it was. He remounted and rode off, presumably in the direction of the gates.

'No,' I replied, 'he's gone away. I presume your brother would come to the house.'

'*Step*brother! I've no wish for a closer relationship. I wonder who it can have been – not that it matters. Have you seen enough now?'

'Oh, do let's stay a little longer, it's so pleasant up here in the fresh air, looking down on the world,' begged Sophie; so we lingered a while until she cried, 'Look, someone's riding up the drive!'

Elinor quickly took up the telescope and peered at the newcomer.

She groaned: 'This time it certainly is Rowland – returning no doubt from heroic deeds at Roscenvalles. Though actually he's more like Tony Lumpkin.'

'I gather you don't like your stepbrother,' said Sophie.

'I like him about as much as he likes me, which is not at all. But then, his mama doesn't like me either. If it wasn't for Papa I don't think I could bear to live here. I was sent away to school when he married again but as I'm now eighteen I can't really stay there any longer. I can't say I liked it much but it was pleasanter than here. And now Rowland has arrived to make my joy complete!'

'Ought we to go down now?' I enquired.

'Oh, there's no hurry on that score. His mama will rush forth to meet him with welcome embraces. She wouldn't leave her study for anyone else, but when Rowland comes home she would kill a fatted calf if she had one.'

When we eventually descended to the ground floor we found Rowland Webb in the library, still submitting to his mother's extravagant greetings. He was a tall, well-built young man of twenty-three, at first glance handsome enough, though on closer inspection I found his portrait had indeed flattered him. His hair, despite Lady Denby's observation, was not gold but straw-coloured and his head was a little too small for his body, tending towards a pineapple shape. The lower part of his face was unappealing; he looked much better with his mouth closed rather than open to its full considerable width, displaying rows of large white teeth.

Lady Denby lost no time in making introductions. She ignored Elinor, who barely acknowledged her stepbrother's arrival before quietly slipping away. Sophie was the focus of our hostess's attention – and of Rowland's too from his first glance. He could scarcely take his eyes off her and seemed eager to further their acquaintance.

'I *knew* you two would be friends!' cried Lady Denby and I felt sure now that this meeting was something she had deliberately contrived. Her husband, Mr Webb, had lost most of his money in foolish investments and was deeply in debt at the time of his death. His widow was forced to leave their handsome home and retire to the nearest town, where she bought a small but respectable property for herself and Rowland. It was a struggle paying his school fees and sending him to Cambridge but she did what was necessary, adding to her limited income by the work of her pen.

Sir Ralph was her saviour and I believe she was genuinely fond of him, but it had begun as a marriage of convenience from her point of view. Although her small income in law belonged to her husband, he not only insisted she keep it all but gave her an extremely generous allowance and showered her with extravagant gifts.

So Rowland must marry well. What better wife than a pretty distant cousin who was sole heiress to a considerable estate? Her ladyship had also ascertained, I had no doubt, that Sophie would bring with her a marriage settlement worth twelve thousand pounds. Amelia Denby could scarcely contain her joy but as I stood a little apart observing the three of them, I detected a certain wariness in Sophie's expression and, just once, an uneasiness in his.

It was a first meeting and I told myself I must not imagine emotions that might not be there. Afterwards, when we went up to change for dinner, I asked Sophie what she thought of Rowland Webb.

'Do you think him handsome?'

'The portrait flatters him but he looks well enough except that he has too many teeth.'

Rowland had come up from London to Ashdale on the Mail. He had left his luggage at the Unicorn to be collected and hired a horse at the livery stables.

The arrival of Rowland's trunk could not, however, account for all the commotion below while we were still in our rooms. There were clatterings and bumpings along corridors, voices and footsteps, doors opening and closing. I concluded the other guests had arrived and our party was now complete. When we went downstairs we were informed that dinner was to be delayed for half an hour as Mrs Thorpe and her nephew Mr Lawrence had just arrived – rather later than expected.

We waited in the Great Hall, where Rowland lost no time

in making himself agreeable to Sophie. George came over to my chair.

'What do you make of him?' he enquired, rather anxiously. 'He and Sophie seem to have hit it off.'

'It's too early to say, but I told you there must be some ulterior motive for our being invited here. Cousin Amelia is wife-hunting for Rowland. I heard quite a lot about him from Elinor. She is, admittedly, prejudiced but not untruthful. I believe he has led a rather dissolute life until now. He left Cambridge without a degree and he's been indulging in riotous living with his London friends. His mother wants to see him settled. Perhaps she thinks marriage would calm him down. I suppose it works with some men. I don't know about *him*.'

George shook his head. 'She's too young. I don't want her heart broken. I'd rather she waited until she was of age and then found some nice steady fellow with money of his own.'

'Well, she can't marry him without your consent – not for nearly four years, anyway.'

'But I don't want to see her hurt.'

'We've all been hurt,' I said softly and he sighed and pressed my hand.

'I saw Hartley riding out of the gates just as I arrived,' said Rowland in his rather loud voice, directing his remark to his stepfather, who was pointing out some item in a magazine to Elinor. 'Has he been visiting?'

'No, not as far as I know,' Sir Ralph replied, 'but Mr Tyler and I were out this afternoon.'

'He didn't call at the house or I would have been informed,' said Lady Denby.

'One of the gardeners probably told him I was out and he

went off home,' said Sir Ralph.

'I suppose that's what happened,' said Rowland. 'He just touched his hat to me but didn't speak. I've always had the feeling Hartley doesn't like me – at least he never talks to me.'

'What nonsense, my dear!' exclaimed Lady Denby. '*Everybody* likes you – how could they not?' She turned to us. 'I'd better explain that Colonel Hartley is our neighbour. He lives at Shelbourne, little more than a mile away. You'll meet him at dinner tomorrow. He dines with us at least once a week.'

'A fine fellow! said Sir Ralph. 'Fought in the Peninsula and at Waterloo.'

I felt sure that the mysterious gentleman I had seen talking to the hermit that afternoon must be Colonel Hartley. Mention of his service under Wellington aroused my interest and I was about to ask for more details when the new arrivals entered the hall.

I took an instant dislike to Louisa Thorpe. Perhaps I instinctively sensed she meant danger. George sprang to his feet and smiled winningly. Mrs Thorpe was exactly the kind of woman he found attractive. He had never realized I knew of his visits to a certain apothecary's widow in our neighbouring market town at home.

Mrs Thorpe was a small, plump, vivacious woman who must have been in her mid-forties if she had been at school with Amelia Denby but she looked considerably younger. She had a generous allowance of dark curls, large, rolling dark eyes to match and a ready, gurgling laugh which seemed to come from the back of her throat.

Her nephew, although as dark as herself, was a different

matter. Frank Lawrence was of medium height and slender build with an expressive face that was not strictly hand-some, but undeniably attractive. He had charm and an easy, assured manner. He was about my own age.

Introductions were made and Lady Denby made it clear she had never met Frank Lawrence before, though she was as effusive in her welcome as usual.

'You are the son of my dear Louisa's eldest sister,' she cooed. 'I believe there's quite a family.'

'Oh, yes – I have three sisters and four brothers,' he smiled.

'I'm so sorry, but I thought your name was Frederick – I remember hearing tales of your exploits at school.'

'I was christened Frederick, certainly, but I never liked the name so I got everyone to call me Frank.'

'But that's short for Francis!' protested Elinor suddenly.

'So it is but Fred is even worse than Frederick.'

'Well, Mr Lawrence,' said Sir Ralph, 'whatever you want to be called I'm sure everyone here will respect your wishes. Liberty Hall – that's what this house is – Liberty Hall!'

I fancied that Lady Denby thought the remark rather vulgar. I wondered, as the evening progressed, whether she might fear Mr Lawrence making overtures to Sophie. He certainly had more polished and engaging manners than Rowland. But although he spoke to my niece in a friendly manner he seemed content to leave her to her first admirer.

To my utter astonishment, Frank Lawrence seemed to direct all his charm towards me. I would have found him easy enough to resist were it not for the fact that he reminded me a little of Harry. Indeed, seen in candlelight across a room he made my heart turn over.

When I retired for the night I looked at Harry's portrait. 'No!' I thought. 'There could never be another!'

# CHAPTER FOUR

I feared George was smitten. There was little I could do except look on helplessly while he made a fool of himself. She was an impoverished widow and he was an eligible, prosperous widower and a pleasant, good-looking man at that. I could only hope that it would not lead to marriage as I knew I could never live under the same roof as Louisa Thorpe. I would have to leave Fairfield. And what of poor Sophie? How would she cope with a stepmother after being the sole focus of her father's affections? She was too old now to send away to school. I let my imagination run on and made myself thoroughly miserable.

The following morning, Mrs Thorpe and her nephew were taken on a tour of the premises. The former had visited Lovegrove before but as everything was new to Frank Lawrence he had to be conducted over the house and allowed to express admiration for its antique splendours. Mrs Thorpe persuaded George to accompany them although he had already taken the tour. I fancied he did not need much encouragement.

I told Sophie to put on her bonnet as I intended to take a walk. There was no sign of Elinor or I would have asked her to come with us. I was just thinking we had escaped Rowland Webb's attentions when he bellowed a greeting from the path behind us and ran to offer us his company.

My heart sank. Rowland was in a cheerful mood and talked a great deal about nothing of consequence. I judged him to be harmless enough; amiable, good-humoured, thoroughly spoilt and not very clever. He had no intellectual interests except perhaps a liking for the theatre, which Sophie shared. His reading had been limited and he had never even managed to finish one of his mother's novels. His world was bounded by horses, dogs, curricles and, I had no doubt, races, prizefights, gambling and other disreputable pursuits.

Sophie was no bluestocking; she liked dancing, pretty clothes and silly romances as much as any other 17-year-old but she deserved better than Rowland. She was far too young to settle down with someone so shallow.

We found ourselves near the hermitage.

'Let's go and explore,' Rowland suggested. 'Old Brother Caspar does a circuit of the park every morning so he won't be back yet.'

'Do you think we ought?' I said. 'It seems very like trespassing.'

But Rowland, ducking his head, led the way through the cave, which did not extend very far, and indicated a door which he flung open. This was the hermit's cell. It consisted of a small, rough-walled room built of undressed stone, a flagged floor and a small window framed in ivy. There was a tiny fireplace with a kettle and a couple of pans, a few items of crockery, a narrow bed covered in a grey blanket, a small crude table and stool and a shelf of books. Everything was very neatly arranged. At the end of the bed stood a trunk with a curved lid.

'Not very interesting,' said Rowland.

'*I* think it's interesting,' said Sophie. 'I never saw a hermit's cell before.'

I was looking at the books: Shakespeare, Byron, Cowper, Gray; several of Scott's novels, a few volumes of history and a number of classical works in Greek and Latin. A small, calf-bound volume lay on the table and I picked it up: *Goldsmith's Poems*. A slip of paper indicated a page about two-thirds of the way through the book. I glanced at it and saw that it had writing on it, and marked a poem called 'The Hermit' which I had never come across before. There was a tiny engraving of a bearded hermit in a long robe, looking remarkably like the inhabitant of this very cell, about to conduct a nervous young traveller thorough a sinister wood.

'I thought you might find this poem very appropriate,' said the message on the paper. The writing was neat and firm and could have been masculine or feminine.

'Look at this!' cried Rowland, picking up a long, battered, brass-bound mahogany box. 'I think I know what this is. Locked, dammit – and look, the nameplate's been removed.'

He showed me the box and there was a discoloured rectangle in the middle of the lid where a brass plate had once carried the initials or name of the owner. I too knew what the box contained. Harry had one very similar.

'But what is it?' asked Sophie. 'Do tell!'

'I think if you wished to inspect my quarters you might have had the courtesy to ask me first,' said a deep, cultivated voice.

The hermit stood in the doorway looking displeased.

Rowland began to bluster.

'Well, no harm done, old fellow. When we've got a hermit on the premises we can't help but feel a bit curious. . . .'

'We're very sorry to intrude,' I said, 'and we shan't bother you again. It was a serious misjudgement on our part.'

'Not at all. Now please leave me to my own devices. I ought not to be talking to you like this.'

I was not merely embarrassed, I was mortified, and hastily made an exit.

Rowland was not greatly troubled. 'Don't know who he thinks he is,' he complained, as we followed the path to the lake. 'He's paid ten guineas a year and all found. What more does he want? He didn't have to take the job. My parents paid for everything in that cell of his.'

'Except his trunk and that mysterious locked box and the books,' said Sophie.

'And that's all he's got in the world so I don't see why he has to demand courtesies from me.'

'I think he's a gentleman,' said Sophie. 'He speaks like one, he carries himself like one and he reads poetry and Greek and Latin.'

'Well, whatever he was before he came here – and I doubt if 'gentleman' would describe it, he's our hermit now – no more than a servant.'

'And you don't know anything about his past?'

'No – Sir Ralph is supposed to be in possession of his real name but I don't think that means very much. He could have given a false one and he didn't tell him much more than that. Who would choose to live as a hermit unless he had some reason to hide away from the world?'

'A broken heart!' cried Sophie. 'Perhaps his wife or

inamorata died.'

'I've never heard of anyone going to such extremes, have you, Miss Tyler?' He directed the question to me.

'No,' I said, 'most people hide their feelings and get on with their everyday lives.'

'Quite! I think there's a much more sinister reason. In fact, I think I know who he may be.'

'Really?' cried Sophie. 'Who?'

'Well, he's obviously done something very seriously wrong – something that might threaten his very life if he were caught. And, as you pointed out, he's educated.'

'Now I remember a notorious case in London a couple of years ago – just before this fellow came here to take up the post of hermit. A barrister called Webster shot his wife. He found out she'd been having an affair with another man. I remember his name because it's so like my own. He disappeared without a trace and hasn't been seen since from that day to this.'

'And you really think your hermit is a murderer?' Sophie was aghast.

'It seems only too likely.'

'But he seems so – so dignified and self-controlled.'

'Who can tell what violent passions may seize a man when in the throes of jealousy – like Othello, you know.'

'He seems so sad and sorrowful.'

'Guilt and remorse!'

I thought Rowland's theory decidedly far-fetched and lurid but whatever Brother Caspar's history might be I felt ashamed of trespassing on his domain. There was some excuse for foolish, impulsive young people like Rowland and Sophie but none at all for me. I decided to write a short apology and wondered if I might give him some small gift to make amends. But what could one give a hermit, dedicated as he was to a simple, ascetic life? It must not be anything of intrinsic value. Perhaps a basket of fruit. . . .

Meanwhile I decided to visit the Lovegrove library and see if I could find a copy of Goldsmith's *Poems*. There was half an hour before lunch; Rowland had taken Sophie off to the stables to see the horses, which seemed an innocent enough activity.

Most of the books in the library had been bought with the house and looked as though no one ever opened them. When I examined the titles I was not surprised. There were whole shelves of bound copies of *The Spectator* and the *Gentleman's Magazine*, dreary law reports and parliamentary proceedings, sermons galore and countless dull works of theology and biblical history. At last I found a section devoted to poetic and dramatic works and discovered a copy of Goldsmith very similar to the one in the hermitage. I soon found 'The Hermit' and settled down to read it, seated comfortably in a high backed chair. I did not realise it screened me from anyone entering the room.

Presently two people came in, deep in conversation. It did not take me long to recognize the voices of my brother and Louisa Thorpe. The tour of the house had obviously come to an end, though apparently Frank had lingered with Sir Ralph, who was explaining to him the finer points of medieval combat.

'Not at all the sort of thing to interest *me*,' said Mrs Thorpe, 'and dear Sir Ralph can be rather tedious at times. Amelia seems quite interested but, of course, such matters may be of use to her when writing her novels. She is related to you, isn't she?'

'Yes. She is second cousin to Charlotte and me. We share great-grandparents.'

So far the conversation was so mundane that I was about to reveal myself but then I realized that to do so would cause us all great embarrassment.

'Oh, dear Mr Tyler, my necklace has come adrift – I fear the clasp has given way. Can you rescue it for me?'

'I'm not very good at this sort of thing but I'll do my best. It's a pity Charlotte isn't here. She's got very agile fingers.'

'Oh no, Mr Tyler, I'm sure you are just as agile – in every possible way!' Her voice was low and seductive. I could scarcely believe my ears, the remark was so blatant – so bold and vulgar. She had not known my brother for a day. I felt sorry for poor George, who was rather a fool where women were concerned. Once or twice I had been obliged to rescue him from some predatory and utterly unsuitable female who saw an agreeable rich man who would perhaps offer matrimony and a life of comfort. If the right woman came along I would not stand in her way but the right woman would certainly not behave like Mrs Thorpe.

'There,' he said, 'I think the clasp is quite securely fastened now. You won't lose your pearls.'

'They are not real ones, I'm afraid. Mr Thorpe left me in a poor way when he died – nothing but a small annuity – everything else to his greedy family, who always hated me. Amelia was left almost as badly off but at least she was able to buy a decent house and she had her writing to sustain her. I was obliged to move to a small cottage and I sold all my jewellery including my real pearls.'

'Well, these are a very good imitation.'

'Do you know how to tell if pearls are real?' she asked.

'Aren't you supposed to bite them or something?'

'Yes, but not really a bite – just slide your teeth over them. Real pearls feel gritty. Fake pearls are smooth. Try it!'

I recalled that her necklace was quite short. I could picture her encouraging my brother to put his mouth close to her neck. There was a certain amount of giggling, chuckling and murmuring: an 'Oh, Mr Tyler!' and a 'Very smooth indeed, Mrs Thorpe!'

I felt nauseated. Then, mercifully, the bell went for luncheon.

# CHAPTER FIVE

Amelia Denby was rather annoyed by a last-minute disruption of her dinner arrangements.

'Eleven at dinner!' she exclaimed. 'That's such an awkward number.'

'Better than thirteen, surely,' said her husband.

Lady Denby ignored him. 'It's too late to invite anyone else to make up the numbers.'

'But you always invite General and Colonel Hartley together,' protested Sir Ralph amiably. 'We know the old man enjoys poor health and can't come very often. We never know until the last minute if he feels up to it. He *is* eighty after all and half-crippled.'

'Yes, in the usual run of things it doesn't matter but it's awkward when I have other guests. Never mind, we'll have to make the best of it and shuffle people round the table.'

Thus it came about that I found myself sitting opposite Louisa Thorpe with the Colonel next to her and Frank Lawrence on my left. As soon as I saw Lieut-Colonel John Hartley, I realized he was indeed the gentleman on horseback I had seen from the roof, talking to the hermit. Then I had thought there was something odd about his appearance.

I had not seen him clearly when he arrived before dinner, as there was some delay helping his father out of the carriage and there was a hasty general introduction before we were all conducted into the dining room.

Now I could see him full face I was momentarily shocked. He had lost his left arm and the empty sleeve was secured to the front of his black evening coat. There was also an ugly puckered scar – a positive furrow – on the left side of his face. He was, I estimated, in his late thirties.

'Like the battered statue of a noble ancient Roman, dug up with a limb missing,' murmured Frank as we took our seats. It was an apposite description.

The Colonel saw me glance at him and smiled. 'Salamanca!' He pointed to his scarred cheek. 'Waterloo!' He indicated his empty sleeve. 'Now we have got that out of the way perhaps we may be friends.'

I watched, fascinated, as he produced a curious implement which combined knife, fork and spoon in one.

'Very useful,' he observed, 'though I know that when I come here everything is discreetly cut up for me.' He turned to Louisa Thorpe. 'I don't think any of us have met prior to this evening,' he said, 'but I do think, Mrs Thorpe, that you have been to this house before.'

'Yes,' she said curtly, then devoted herself to cooing at Sir Ralph, who was presiding over that end of the table.

'Ah, that must have been when I was away from home or I would certainly have remembered you.' The Colonel still smiled but there was a note of irony in his voice.

Fortunately Frank Lawrence had much to say on a variety of subjects and the meal passed very agreeably.

Later, in the drawing room, after the gentlemen joined us,

I found myself, to my distaste, next to Louisa Thorpe.

'I really must complain to Amelia about placing me next to that Colonel Hartley,' she declared. 'It wouldn't have been so bad if his good side had been towards me but I got the empty sleeve and that horrid scar. It made me feel quite sick.' She rolled her eyes expressively.

'It's just as well the rest of the country feels nothing but gratitude for those brave men who have made such sacrifices for us,' I said, with some feeling.

She rose at once, quite deliberately without a word, and took herself off to the other side of the room where George and Frank were deep in conversation. Even if I had not disliked her before, this small incident would have turned me against her. As it was, it served to increase my animosity.

'Well spoken, my dear,' said a deep voice close to my ear. 'I'm glad my son has such a spirited defender. Do you mind if I sit beside you?' It was the tall, cadaverous old gentleman whom I understood to be Colonel Hartley's father. He leaned heavily on his stick and sank slowly onto the sofa as I hastily moved a cushion out of the way.

'Are you quite comfortable, sir?' I asked.

'As comfortable as I'm ever likely to be. I rarely venture out for dinner these days. But this hot weather seems to suit me. The cold eats into my bones and makes my old wounds ache. It's pleasant to experience a change of scene and meet new people. I take it you are here with your brother, Mr Tyler?'

'Yes, and with my niece Sophie. Lady Denby is a cousin and she invited us.'

He nodded. 'I'm glad to see Lovegrove inhabited again. I knew Miss Wilton, the last of her family. She lived on here until she was over ninety with most of the house closed down and going to rack and ruin. The Denbys have brought it back to life.'

I reflected that he probably had very little in common with Sir Ralph and his wife but he seemed to appreciate their efforts to restore the priory. 'You must be glad to have your son at home again after all his adventures,' I said.

'Oh, yes. We're a military family of course and used to long separations but I am relieved John didn't go to India with his regiment. I'm sure I would never have seen him again. Besides, he was needed here on the estate. There's no one else. I lost my other son in Spain.'

'Where?' I enquired.

'Ciudad Rodrigo.'

'I was engaged to an officer who was killed in the assault on Badajos.'

'Ah, sieges are the very devil. What regiment?'

'The Rifles.'

'The first in the field and the last out of it. The bloody, fighting ninety-fifth!'

'Harry was in one of the storming parties so he would certainly have been among the first in, but he never came out of it.'

He regarded me for a moment with a searching look and then his bony hand closed over mine. 'We have both suffered great losses which no one else in this room could possibly understand.'

I felt tears in my eyes.

'Particularly not,' he added, 'that very silly woman you put down so successfully. And now, my dear, I see that handsome young man is hovering in the hope of taking my place.

I will go and talk to Sir Ralph about the hay harvest. I'm sure you have had enough of an old man's conversation.'

'Oh, no!' I assured him, 'I do hope we can talk again.'

He smiled, patted my hand and heaved himself to his feet assisted by Frank Lawrence who, as he had observed, was waiting to sit beside me.

'I am afraid I find my aunt a little tiresome occasionally,' he said. 'I enjoyed talking to your brother. She seems to have taken a fancy to him.'

'I'm afraid so.'

We turned and saw the happy couple; Louisa Thorpe clinging to George's arm as though glued there, his head bent to hear the words she was murmuring in his ear.

Sophie was playing the piano with Rowland beside her. When she had finished we all applauded politely. It was competent at least. Then she was prevailed upon to accompany Rowland who, his mother informed us, had a magnificent voice and in humbler circumstances could have been an opera singer. It was a decent enough baritone – better than I anticipated if truth be told. Lady Denby's praises always made me expect the worst.

Then Elinor was coerced into accompanying Sophie and Rowland in a duet. My niece had a sweet, rather tremulous voice but sounded well enough with male support.

'As we are enjoying singing this evening,' Lady Denby informed us, 'we have saved the best until last. Louisa dear, can I persuade you to entertain us?'

I caught a glimpse of Elinor, still at the piano, looking vindictive but she rapidly brought her countenance under control.

Louisa's voice really was very good indeed: rich, warm and

expressive. She first gave us a plaintive Italian song, then a Scottish ballad and ended with a sprightly French ditty. George applauded enthusiastically when she had finished. I noticed Colonel Hartley slapping the arm of his chair.

'She *is* good, isn't she?' said Frank.

'Remarkably so. She is very talented.'

'In more ways than one. Oh, I know – she's a tremendous flirt.'

'If it were only flirtation it wouldn't matter but I'm afraid she's set her cap at my brother. He's somewhat susceptible to attractive brunettes with dimples.'

'Yes, she's a pretty woman for her age but she's my aunt. I prefer looks of a different sort.' He gazed at me with undisguised admiration.

'Really?' I said, as evenly as possible. 'It's rather odd in George's case because his wife was blonde like Sophie and he was utterly devoted to her. Of course, they weren't married very long and he's never shown any inclination to find anyone else.'

'Frank, do come over and sing for us!' cried Mrs Thorpe. 'Here's a surprise for you all! You've never heard my nephew and he has the most charming voice.'

I wondered if this was a ploy to get him away from me, but after an initial display of reluctance, he went over to the piano and sang one of Thomas Moore's Irish melodies. It was Harry's favourite.

'The Minstrel Boy to the war is gone.

In the ranks of death you will find him. . . .'

It was a light tenor voice and very expressive. I had some difficulty controlling my feelings.

When he had finished and declined to sing an encore

Colonel Hartley came over to me. I thought that Frank looked momentarily annoyed to see his place taken but my attention was immediately seized by the Colonel's first remark: 'My father tells me you were engaged to an officer of the 95th who was killed at Badajos. It wasn't Harry O'Neill by any chance?'

I was already unnerved by the song. Now I must have changed countenance for he caught my hand in his.

'I'm sorry if I startled you but—'

'No, it was the shock of hearing his name so suddenly and unexpectedly. I didn't think you'd have heard of him.'

'The whole army heard of Harry O'Neill. You see, we were like a great big family – everyone knew everybody else, more or less. And Lord Wellington was like a stern parent directing us all. Any particularly colourful personalities became widely known. Harry was incredibly brave and daring – adored by his men – always in the forefront. I knew he'd got engaged to a girl back in England during his sick leave and was desperate for promotion.'

'I feel guilty sometimes. He wanted so much to get his majority so that we could afford to marry at the end of the war. Perhaps he wouldn't have been so reckless if—'

'No, set your mind at rest. Harry O'Neill would have done what he did in any circumstances. That is how he was. He was a great loss to his regiment.'

'Thank you so much for telling me this. I'm so glad he's remembered by others.'

'He's remembered by everyone who fought with him and I'm sure Wellington himself has not forgotten him.'

'That is a great comfort. But you had your own sorrow – you lost your brother.'

'Yes, I don't think my poor father has ever got over it. It was worse for him and I don't just mean that losing a son is worse than losing a brother however strong the affection might be. I was so occupied that I had little time for grief. I found Tom's body and saw he had a decent burial. Then we moved on – and my father was at home alone, in declining health and wondering if I would survive the war.'

'You must miss the army,' I said.

'Well, times like those won't ever come again. There won't ever be another army under another commander like that. I've become a country squire and it's nice to know I'm not likely to be killed tomorrow. I haven't got to march at dawn or sleep in a damp bivouac. One gets used to comfort in time as one got used to hardship.'

'Elinor is about to play,' I said. 'We must listen – she has a great gift far beyond the amateur efforts of the others.'

'I agree. Not that I know a great deal about music – but she deserves our attention.'

We continued to sit side by side on the sofa and I felt a comfortable closeness to Colonel Hartley. He had known Harry and led the life that he had led.

When Elinor had finished and been applauded, I remarked to my companion that the room had become stiflingly hot. It was a very warm night and the heat of the many candles made it worse.

'You are right,' he said, 'the windows aren't open far enough.' He rose and I followed him as it occurred to me that a one-armed man might find it difficult to raise a sash.

'Perhaps we can manage it between us,' I suggested.

'What a helpful young lady you are,' he smiled.

When we had accomplished our task we stood for a while

enjoying the cool air and the view of the park bathed in moonlight. I suddenly realized that a figure was sitting on the stone bench against the wall below – a hooded figure which rose and glided away even as we watched.

'It's the hermit!' I exclaimed. 'He must have been sitting there listening to the music.'

'Well, he loves music and this is the only chance he has to hear anything.'

'You know him?'

'Oh yes, it was through me he obtained the post of hermit. A ridiculous occupation but it suits him very well.'

'But you know who he is?'

'Yes, I know who he is. Even Sir Ralph doesn't know that – but I can't tell anyone. I gave my word.'

I thought of Rowland Webb's idea that the hermit might be a barrister who had shot his wife. Somehow it now seemed even more unlikely.

# CHAPTER SIX

'Today,' announced Lady Denby next morning, 'as the gentlemen are all riding over to a cricket match at Somerwick I
thought we ladies would take a little outing to Ashdale. It's
market day and there are some tolerable shops and a fine old
church that's worth inspecting. I've arranged for us to have
a cold collation in a private room at the Unicorn and in the
afternoon we can drive to Hollingstone to admire the view.
Then we can return home at our leisure.'

'But your novel, dear Amelia!' exclaimed Louisa Thorpe. 'I
thought you could not leave it.'

'Some sacrifices have to be made when one has guests,'
observed Lady Denby. 'Besides, I've reached an impasse. I
must rest from my labours for a day or two to refresh my
imagination.'

This arrangement met with everyone's approval. The gentlemen rode off after breakfast and a little later the barouche
was brought round for the females of the party. When we
reached the small market town of Ashdale we divided. Lady
Denby and Mrs Thorpe went off together and Sophie and I
found ourselves joined by Elinor.

'Do you mind if I come with you?' she asked. 'I feel like an intruder with those two and they treat me with such conde-scension I could scream.'

'Not at all,' I said. 'I'm sure you belong with the younger half of the party.'

We strolled round the shops and through the busy market where I bought a small basket and filled it with oranges, strawberries and cherries.

'We have plenty of fruit at home,' said Elinor, rather mystified.

'It's by way of an apology to Brother Caspar,' I explained. 'We intruded on his privacy the other day and I thought I'd leave a small offering outside his cave. What do you make of him?'

'I don't know.' Elinor seemed unwilling to say more.

'Something very sad – perhaps even tragic – has hap-pened to him, I'm sure,' I said.

'Rowland thinks he's a London barrister who murdered his wife,' said Sophie.

'That is exactly the sort of thing Rowland *would* say!' Elinor sounded positively vicious. 'He has no understanding of other people – particularly those more intelligent than himself – and that means at least half the population.'

'Well, I'm sure your hermit is no criminal,' I said. 'I suspect he is an army acquaintance of Colonel Hartley. Apparently he found him the post but he is unwilling to say more. Perhaps he suffered greatly in the war and sought refuge in peaceful surroundings.'

'He can't have suffered more than Colonel Hartley,' said Sophie.

'There is more than one kind of suffering,' observed Elinor.

'True,' I agreed, thinking of General Hartley and his grief for his dead son.

The rest of the morning passed pleasantly. We dutifully visited the church, which was very fine and contained some interesting monuments. At half past twelve we repaired to the Unicorn Inn for our cold collation. It was a fine, large hostelry situated in the market square and we were conducted to a comfortable room on the first floor with windows looking out on the bustling market below.

The meal was simple but excellent and we lingered, chatting in a desultory fashion.

'I can hear a baby crying!' said Elinor suddenly.

'Oh, there's always a hullaballoo in an inn like this,' declared Lady Denby, 'so many people are coming and going all the time.'

Eventually we took ourselves downstairs to the inn yard where our carriage was waiting. Elinor abruptly announced that she had left her reticule in the dining room so she excused herself and ran upstairs to fetch it. She was gone such a long time that Lady Denby asked me to go after her.

'What can the girl be doing?' she complained. 'This is a rambling sort of building but I hardly think she could have got lost.'

I was halfway up the stairs when I encountered Elinor coming down. It seemed obvious at once that something had upset her. I had never seen her so flushed and agitated.

'Are you all right?' I asked.

'Yes of course. I – I couldn't find my reticule. It wasn't where I thought I'd left it. I have it now. That's all!' I didn't believe her.

We enjoyed an uneventful drive to Hollingstone where I

made a few sketches and dutifully admired the view over five counties and then we headed home. Throughout the excursion Elinor scarcely spoke and seemed preoccupied. I was sure she had seen something or met somebody on her return indoors at the inn, but she was obviously not going to confide in anyone.

On our return to Lovegrove I decided to take my basket of fruit to the hermitage before going up to my room. I had written a brief note of apology which I tucked in among the fruit. I intended to leave it at the entrance to the cave but just as I put it in place, the door to the cell opened and Brother Caspar emerged.

I was somewhat disconcerted but could not walk away without some explanation.

'A small gift . . .' I indicated the basket. 'I much regretted our intrusion yesterday. It was my fault. The others are young and heedless. I should have prevented them entering.'

'Think no more of it – I doubt if you could have done anything. The young are wilful and opposition makes them worse.'

'I wasn't sure if you were committed to an austere monkish diet but I thought fruit would be acceptable.'

'Anything is acceptable. Thank you! I am sure Lady Denby would like me to subsist on spring water and herbs,' (I caught a direct reference to Goldsmith's poem) 'but I don't think I'd survive long on that. I get two meals a day from the house and Colonel Hartley brings me an occasional treat – a bottle of wine or the like. I do very well. He also keeps me supplied with books so I am never bored.'

'Did you enjoy the music last night?'

He started a little. 'You saw me?'

'Colonel Hartley and I were at the window and saw you leave. He said you loved music and this was the only chance you had to hear it.'

'True.'

'And Miss Denby plays very well.'

'Remarkably so.'

'Colonel Hartley said he had found you this post but he wouldn't tell me anything about you. This is a very lonely life you have chosen.'

'Solitary rather than lonely. It suits my disposition. John Hartley is the best of friends and the best of men.'

He picked up the basket and gave a small bow which looked odd coming from a man in a monkish robe but I realized he must once have dressed normally and mixed in society.

'I mustn't keep you here,' he said 'they'll be having dinner up at the house and one of the servants will be bringing me my tray. Good evening and thank you for the gift.'

The door closed behind him and I went back to the house. The hermit was certainly a gentleman. Surely he had a family and friends who must wonder what had become of him. It was difficult to judge his age, especially with all that greying hair and beard, but I fancied he was younger than he looked.

At dinner, less than an hour later, there was some talk of the cricket match.

'Where did you get to, Rowland?' enquired Sir Ralph. 'You disappeared for a couple of hours.'

'I got bored and rode over to Creswood. I wanted to see a horse Tom Radley has for sale.'

'Are you going to buy it?'

'No, it's sway-backed.'

As usual Frank Lawrence paid a great deal of attention to me but I could not take him seriously. He had no prospects and I knew only too well what could result from that. I wished with all my heart I had married Harry. He would still have died; we would have had only a few weeks together but I felt I could have lived off that for the rest of my life. At least Harry had a purpose to his life; he was passionately devoted to the army and his regiment. Frank seemed rootless and restless, lacking in ambition. He was certainly pleasant company, witty and entertaining with a fund of stories about his life in the militia and a brief career on a merchant ship, a spell with a wine merchant and journeys abroad as a courier.

'I thought, from something Lady Denby said, that you were originally destined for the Church,' I said.

'Indeed I was but can you see me as a clergyman?'

'Not really.'

'Neither could I – besides which, I was never much of a scholar – I've always preferred action to study.'

'I got the impression you were a great reader.'

'Oh, I'd hardly call myself that. A *wide* reader would be a better description – but mostly novels, plays, poetry – some history but nothing too demanding.'

'Mr Lawrence!' cried Lady Denby. 'If I can tear you away from the delightful Miss Tyler, do you think I could persuade you to give us another of your sweet Irish songs? Just *one*,' she added as he seemed to hesitate, 'before the card tables are set up. It will put us in the right frame of mind.'

I was not at all sure what she meant by that, though it was obvious she wanted to remove Frank from his seat beside me on the sofa for as he went over to the piano she took his place, smiling at me winningly.

He began singing and he seemed to be directing the words to me:

'She is far from the land where her young hero sleeps,

And lovers around her are sighing:

But coldly she turns from their gaze and weeps

For her heart in his grave is lying . . .'

I had felt like that for many years, though I had never attracted any sighing lovers. But the grief had worn itself out; I knew that when I moved Harry's ring to my right hand. Did Frank Lawrence know about Harry O'Neill? If so, the only way he could have come by the knowledge was if my brother had carelessly dropped a word to Mrs Thorpe, who had passed it on to her nephew. I was growing increasingly exasperated with George.

'You look very pensive my dear,' said Lady Denby when he had finished. 'Does that song have a particular meaning for you?'

'Not at all.' I wondered why she was suddenly so interested in me and suspected she was seeking a favour. This proved to be the case. On hearing I was an amateur artist and having observed me sketching on our trip to Hollingstone she asked if I could draw portraits of each of her guests during our stay.

I agreed readily enough. Most people enjoy having their likeness taken. Having fetched my sketchbook, I began that evening with a study of Lady Denby which greatly pleased her.

'I shall have an album put together,' she declared, 'and it will be a delightful souvenir of this party.'

I never realized how important my collection of portraits would prove to be.

# CHAPTER SEVEN

The fine weather continued and two days later we all set off on an expedition to Normaston Castle, which was about eight miles away and where we were to have a picnic. We ladies travelled in the carriage and the gentlemen, including Colonel Hartley, accompanied us on horseback.

The castle was a picturesque ruin of the sort beloved by Lady Denby. 'Situate upon an eminence,' she sighed, 'a veritable scene of romance.'

It was certainly picturesque and I had brought with me my sketchbook and watercolours. I tried to persuade Sophie to do likewise as she had some talent but she was a reluctant artist, lacking patience and perseverance. I suspected she was hoping to wander about with Rowland as she seemed to enjoy his company. She still made disparaging remarks about him, especially if I questioned her concerning her attitude; but I feared she was growing to like him. I hoped it was a sisterly affection such as I had for George but I was not at all sure.

The party split up and we went off to explore the ruins, Lady Denby and Sir Ralph pointing out arches, stairways and towers, all smothered in brambles and ivy.

I eventually found a spot near a wall with an attractive aspect for me to draw. I flattened some tall weeds, spread my shawl and settled down with my pencil and sketchbook. I was rather hoping that Frank Lawrence might join me and amuse me with his lively conversation but he was nowhere to be seen.

For some time I was absorbed in my occupation, but then I realized that there were two people on the other side of the wall and they seemed to be arguing. I thought I ought to move but I was comfortably settled and it would take a few minutes to gather all my belongings together. Perhaps they would go away.

'You're making a perfect fool of yourself.' It was Frank's voice.

'What right have you to criticize me?' his aunt demanded furiously. 'Neither Mr Tyler nor I are married. He would probably make a very good husband – rich, quite handsome, very easy-going and amiable. A good deal nicer than Thorpe, I can tell you.'

'Don't provoke me.'

'I'll provoke whoever I please. And for that matter, aren't you rather overdoing your attentions to that dull Tyler girl? She has no money, no prospects and is obviously condemned to spinsterhood.'

'She's by no means dull and as you've scarcely spoken to her I don't know how you can tell. She's actually quite lively and amusing. I find her decidedly attractive and she's a good fifteen years younger than you.'

'Miss Tyler is thirty if she's a day, and looks it. If I were to marry her brother, I'd soon get rid of her.'

'I advise you not to continue your pursuit of him.'

'Advise all you like. What can you possibly do about it?'

Then there was silence. One or the other – probably both – had stormed off in a temper. I found it a curious conversation and not because it contained some frank opinions of George and me but on account of the general tone, which was surprisingly intense and intimate for an exchange between aunt and nephew. It was more like a lovers' quarrel. Something rather unsavoury there, I thought, and I was not at all happy about her possible intentions towards my brother. A flirtation seemed in danger of slipping over into something far more serious.

'Ah, there you are!' At first I felt a momentary annoyance at my solitude being interrupted and then I saw it was Colonel Hartley. I could not possibly be displeased with him.

'I hope I'm not disturbing you.'

'Of course not, I'll be glad of your company. Did you happen to see Sophie?'

'She's wandering about with Rowland, which should please Lady Denby, though I'm not sure about you.'

'He's not good enough for her and she's too young to know her own mind. I don't want to see her take up with the first personable young man she encounters. I'm not sure if he's a fortune-hunter.'

'I think not, but I'm sure his mother is, to say nothing of her dear friend Mrs Thorpe. You don't like her, do you?'

'Not at all and I fear for my poor brother.'

'She has her claws into him, I can see that, but he seems a willing victim.'

'I wish I could do something about it but he wouldn't listen to me. He can be very stubborn. It's not the first time some unsuitable woman has made overtures, but on previous occasions they weren't living under the same roof and seeing him every day. Nor were they as beautiful as Mrs Thorpe.'

'Not the sort of beauty that greatly appeals to me. I saw enough brunettes in Spain and there were times when I longed for light hair and an English complexion.'

He asked to see my sketches, made appreciative remarks and the conversation slipped into easier channels. I asked if I might add his portrait to my collection and he assented good-humouredly. 'On condition that it's my good side.'

'Of course – if you will be kind enough to keep quite still for a few minutes.'

I sketched his right profile and showed him the result when I had finished.

'You've made me too handsome,' he observed.

I looked at my work critically. 'Yes, possibly, but it will have to do.'

'Oh, you disappoint me, Miss Tyler. I hoped you'd assure me that it was a very good likeness.'

'I don't flatter people, Colonel Hartley.'

'I'm sure you don't. And neither do I.'

He talked for a while of his life in the army and I was able to compare his experiences with Harry's.

'How did you meet Harry O'Neill?' he asked. 'I thought he was Irish.'

'So he was. His father was a country doctor in County Clare. There was a large family of boys – all in the army or navy. His only sister married an English doctor and came to live in Whitcombe, our nearest town. After Harry's father died his mother was invited to live with them. When Harry was wounded at Sabugal and sent home to recover, it was only natural for him to stay at the doctor's house where he could receive medical treatment and be nursed back to health by his mother and sister.'

'So you met him in Whitcombe?'

'Yes, in a ball at the Assembly Rooms. He asked me to stand up with him but he wasn't at all well and nearly collapsed. I helped him to a seat and gave him my smelling salts – the reversal of the faint young lady being assisted by her gallant partner. We laughed about it afterwards. Poor Harry! He was so full of life and he hated being ill but if he hadn't been wounded I would never have met him.

'Eventually we were seeing each other nearly every day and became engaged before he rejoined his regiment.'

'And your brother approved?'

'Oh yes, he liked Harry very much but he warned me that neither of us had any money and we ought not to marry until our situation improved. He was right, of course, but I still wish we'd gone ahead and married anyway.'

'At least you've the satisfaction of having won the love of a man like Harry O'Neill.' He paused a moment and then added softly, 'And I begin to understand why.'

Had I heard right? Had I misunderstood? But he had returned to examining my sketches.

At that point one of the servants rang a bell to summon all the party back to the place designated for our picnic. George already lay stretched out on the grass with a slice of pigeon pie and a glass of wine in front of him. Louisa Thorpe sat beside him under her parasol, very animated and treating him like a child to be fed and pampered. He was enjoying the attention.

Colonel Hartley was about to sit beside me when somehow Frank Lawrence cut in and threw himself down on the grass. The Colonel quietly withdrew and went to the other end of the group.

'It's confounded hot!' Frank complained, flinging off his hat and revealing the dark curls that so resembled Harry's. The Colonel's hair was plentiful enough but a commonplace mouse-brown and of the sort that always looks dishevelled.

'I envy you ladies in your muslins. You all look so cool. I think we shall have a thunderstorm before we've finished. What have you been doing with yourself? I was looking for you.'

'Sketching and painting.' I was about to say I'd left my materials in the shade of a certain wall but I stopped myself just in time. He might realise I had overheard an intimate conversation. I glanced round and saw that Colonel Hartley was seated between Elinor and Sophie, with Rowland and the Denbys to the other side and George and Mrs Thorpe next to us.

I found my feelings towards Frank had changed a little since my accidental eavesdropping. I felt rather uneasy and wondered what his relationship with his aunt might be.

'All on your own?' He helped himself to a plate of ham. 'I wish I'd known.'

'No, Colonel Hartley was with me.'

'Oh, 'Armless 'Artley – you won't have any trouble from him.'

It was a coarse remark and a cruel one. I said nothing but did not laugh and he realized, after a few minutes silence, that he had gone too far.

'I meant no offence,' he muttered. 'I'm sure the Colonel's a very good fellow.'

'He hardly requires your patronage,' I snapped,

thoroughly annoyed by him.

George was lying back laughing as Louisa Thorpe tickled his face with a long piece of grass.

'Really, Louisa!' boomed Lady Denby. 'Do leave poor Mr Tyler alone. He'll never finish his pie if you continue to torment him.'

Mrs Thorpe pretended she had not heard and I began to feel both irritated and depressed. What should have been a happy day proved to be too full of tension to be wholly enjoyable. Yet there was one small circumstance that made up for everything. I could see that Colonel Hartley was deep in conversation with Elinor. He looked up suddenly and smiled at me and then raised his wine glass towards me in a silent toast.

# CHAPTER EIGHT

That night the weather broke. Thunder rolled, lightning flashed and I heard heavy rain drenching the parched earth. I slept badly and woke unrefreshed. The morning was dark, the rain still fell and I realized we were all destined to spend the day indoors.

At breakfast Sir Ralph declared it was a perfect day for showing us his collection in the Long Gallery. Rowland, Elinor and Mrs Thorpe excused themselves from the tour as they had seen it all before. The rest of us obligingly trooped up to the top floor, along creaking old passages, to the gallery, which ran the full length of the house, the long windows letting in as much light as possible on such a dull day.

Sir Ralph was an enthusiastic collector but not a discriminating one. My second examination of the exhibits confirmed my first impression formed on our initial visit at the beginning of our stay at Lovegrove. There never was such an accumulation of rubbish and genuine curiosities. What is more, the items were displayed in confusion with little attempt to separate the exhibits. Cabinets full of medallions and cameos jostled with halberds, crossbows and helmets. Matting from the Sandwich Islands was displayed next to cases of mineral specimens. Suits of armour were mixed up with fragments of Roman statuary, Greek vases and bits of tapestry.

A glass box contained a lock of Mary Queen of Scot's hair.

'My heroine!' breathed Lady Denby.

I did not tell her I had always thought her a very silly woman.

I tried to let my eye pick out a few things to study properly and let the rest fade into the background; bits of rusty metal and dusty rhinoceros horn did not interest me.

This lasted until eleven and after that the party dispersed. Lady Denby retired to her study to work on her novel but I did not stay to see what the others were doing. I was determined to do a little exploring on my own as there were parts of the house that I had scarcely seen.

Eventually I found myself in the Tapestry Room, an unoccupied bedroom full of Tudor and Stuart furniture and, as its name implied, lined with faded tapestries telling biblical stories. I tried to decipher them and identified Abraham about to slay Isaac and David holding up the head of the dead Goliath. Everything else was too frayed and blurred by age to make out.

Suddenly I heard a sound that made me turn cold: a muffled moaning. I remembered that this room was supposed to be haunted by a Lady Chater who appeared, moaning and sighing for her husband who had been carried off to the Tower. I almost expected to see a grey apparition in Tudor dress.

I stood frozen to the spot. The moaning continued, followed by a small shriek and then a man's voice and a woman's laughter. It was impossible to hear any actual words but certainly there were two people very close – not in the room itself and not, I thought, next door, but . . .

I moved round the room, listening at the walls, and at last found a portion of the tapestry which was not secured by pegs at its base. On lifting it up I found a door let into the panelling. I was about to knock and then changed my mind. Someone was still murmuring and laughing on the other side of the door and I feared an embarrassing confrontation. I hastily slipped out of the room and went up to the Long Gallery to seek diversion from the collection.

However, my curiosity had been aroused and I continued to wonder who had been in the closet – for that is what I thought might be on the other side of the door under the tapestry. It could well be that two of the servants were using the concealed room for a dalliance. A pretty word, that – all nymphs and shepherds and hey nonny nonny! I felt sure the truth was more mundane and perhaps sordid.

I could not resist returning to the Tapestry Room about an hour later. I entered cautiously, listening at the door before I went in, but everything was quiet. Then I lifted up the tapestry and stood for a while at the inner door, but I heard nothing. Slowly I opened the latch and peered inside but to my relief no one was there. I noticed there was a crude wooden bolt to secure the room against intruders. It was scarcely a room at that – indeed, my supposition that it was a closet seemed correct as it was less than twelve feet by twelve and was illuminated only by one tiny window which rattled in the wind and let in a dim, greenish light through a veil of ivy.

The furniture consisted of a huge chest that could have

served as an altar when the house belonged to a Catholic family, and also a day bed, an old red velvet close stool, a small table and a chair. That was all, apart from the cushions; and there were many of those, on the bed and on the floor. They had a crushed and crumpled look, as though in recent use.

I searched the closet for some evidence of its recent occupants but found nothing but a solitary hairpin which might have been dropped by anyone at any time. Yet a musky scent lingered, especially on one of the cushions. Both Lady Denby and Louisa Thorpe were heavily perfumed but my suspicions were immediately directed to the latter. As to her partner in the liaison – here I felt sick; only one man was it likely to be and that was my poor susceptible brother.

Before leaving, I moved the two heavy brass candlesticks from the top of the chest and raised the lid. It was half-full of old, musty damask curtains and a faded velvet counterpane.

On my return to my room I encountered Sophie at her door, about to enter.

'Have you had a pleasant morning?' I asked.

'Pleasant enough. Rowland and I played carpet bowls in the library.'

'Alone?'

'More or less but the door was open and we were interrupted a few times. Lady Denby came in for a book.'

'Did she say anything?'

'Oh, she beamed on us and said we seemed to be getting on very well.'

'Yes, she would. How do you feel about Rowland?'

'I like him better than I did. He's quite good company and doesn't sulk if he doesn't win.'

'I trust he knows how to behave himself.'

'Of course he does. He hasn't tried to kiss me, if that's what you mean.'

'Not quite, but don't let him. So you spent the whole time on bowls?'

'No, we tired of it after a while and went looking for the lost priest-hole, tapping the wainscot all round the house. Rowland says the other priest-hole is bigger than the one I went down and is supposed to open onto a passage to the priory ruins.'

'I presume you didn't find anything of interest?'

'Of course not, but it was fun searching.'

'Did you happen to see your father?' I sounded as unconcerned as possible.

'Papa? No, I don't know where he was. Did you want to see him for anything?'

'Not particularly. He'll be at luncheon anyway.'

So he was and after the meal I managed to speak to George briefly.

'I trust you enjoyed your morning?' I said sardonically.

'You mean after seeing the collection?' Well, rather boring if truth be told. What can one do indoors on such a day?'

'What indeed? What did you do?'

He shrugged. 'Nothing of consequence. Why the questions? I might well ask you what you were doing.'

There was nothing to be gained from such an exchange. I could scarcely reproach George even if I knew for sure that it had been him in the closet with Mrs Thorpe. I was entirely dependent on him and had no right to criticize his behaviour to his face whatever misgivings I might have in private.

I began to long for the peace and quiet of Fairfield. Only

one thing made me want to prolong our sojourn at Lovegrove. The Denbys, however, obviously intended our visit to be extended indefinitely; George seemed more than happy to stay on and Sophie was enjoying herself.

The two young men were understandably more restless. Frank Lawrence announced that he had promised to stay with some friends in Derby for a few days, so off he went. A day later Rowland said he intended to visit a Cambridge friend in the next county who had a horse for sale. He would probably be gone for a day or two. I fancy his mother was rather annoyed by this as she saw it as an interruption to his courtship of Sophie but I heard him say in a loud whisper, 'Don't worry Mama, absence makes the heart grow fonder.'

Without Frank and Rowland the atmosphere of the party changed subtly. Perhaps this was due to women now out-numbering men. Louisa Thorpe could continue her pursuit of George without the critical eye of her nephew. Sophie noticed it too and remarked that she disliked that Thorpe woman, who seemed far too interested in Papa.

'She'd never succeed in marrying him, though – he'd never give me a stepmother I hated.'

I was not so sure.

It seemed to me that Sophie missed Rowland a little; she seemed restless and bored despite efforts to amuse her. One morning I borrowed the Denbys' gig and drove her into Ashdale. We had, of course, been there before with Lady Denby but shops are always an attraction for girls and we had more time and freedom on our own.

'Look!' cried Sophie. 'Isn't that Rowland Webb at that cottage door?'

A tall young man in a bright blue coat and buff breeches

stood with his back to us on the other side of the street. It certainly looked like him from the rear. The door opened and he removed his hat, revealing fair hair cut in the most fashionable style.

'Can it really be Rowland?' said Sophie. 'He's supposed to be visiting a Cambridge friend near Nottingham.'

'He could have come over here for some reason. Perhaps we can find out who lives there,' I said.

The opportunity arose when we visited a milliner's shop only a few doors away from the cottage. Sophie bought a new straw bonnet and I engaged the shop's proprietor in conversation.

'We thought we saw a friend visiting one of the cottages a little further along from here – a green front door. Probably a charitable errand. Do you know who lives there?'

'That would be Mrs Deane. She takes in lodgers. She's only got one at the moment – a young woman, I believe.'

Sophie looked up at me, shocked. 'We could have been mistaken, of course.'

'I'm sure we were.' But I remembered Elinor's strange behaviour at the Unicorn and wondered if there was any connection.

Several days passed by and the weather settled again, though not as hot as before. For me the most enjoyable events of that time were my occasional meetings with Colonel Hartley. He came to dinner again, as he did regularly every week, and on another afternoon we drove over to dinner at his house. Shelbourne was less than a hundred years old and not particularly large or interesting compared with Lovegrove but I liked it far better. It was light and cheerful and although portraits of Colonel Hartley's dead wife and son reminded us of tragedy, the atmosphere was not overlaid with ancient gloom.

'I could live here quite happily,' I thought and hastily told myself I was thinking about the house and not its inhabitants.

Frank returned and so, a day later, did Rowland. The latter was asked if he had bought the horse that interested him.

'No – I tried riding him but he didn't handle well. Not worth what Logan was asking.'

'But you had a pleasant few days?' enquired Lady Denby.

'Well enough.'

'We've all missed you,' she declared, adding with coy emphasis, 'especially *one* of us!'

Sophie blushed but Rowland avoided looking at her and said he was confoundedly dusty and needed a wash.

Frank Lawrence also seemed to have enjoyed his excursion. At the first opportunity he drew me to one side and presented me with a little brown paper package.

'To prove I did not forget you while I was away,' he smiled. 'You were rather cross with me that day at Normaston, and rightly so. I spoke out of turn, I'm afraid. I sometimes let my tongue run away with me and I always regret it. What I said was not intended to offend. Am I forgiven?'

'Of course, but you shouldn't have bought me anything. I'm not sure it's at all proper.'

'Wait until you see what it is.'

It was a small book, beautifully bound: *Goldsmith's Essays*.

'It's perfectly in order to give a lady a book. I saw you

reading Goldsmith's *Poems* and thought this an appropriate companion piece.'

'Of course it is. Thank you!'

Out of the corner of my eye I caught sight of Louisa Thorpe across the room glaring at us both with a venomous expression.

'You couldn't have pleased me more,' I said. 'Perhaps you'll let me draw your portrait. You know I'm providing likenesses of the party for Lady Denby as a souvenir of our visit.'

'Anything you want, my dear Miss Tyler. If it involves sitting beside you on the sofa I'm only too happy to oblige.'

He kissed my hand and I smiled and made sure that Mrs Thorpe saw me smile.

There was only one unusual incident which occurred in the quiet days following the return of the two young men. One night I could not sleep. The stable clock chimed the hours and it was two in the morning when I finally rose and went over to the window. I thought if I enjoyed a few minutes of fresh air it might put me in the mood for sleep.

It was very quiet but in the country that never means absolute silence. There were distant rustlings and scufflings, the cry of an owl, the scream of some wild creature and then – two shots rang out, one after the other.

I mentioned this to Sir Ralph the following morning.

'I suppose it was the gamekeepers in the park but I thought I'd better tell you.'

'They're not supposed to be in the park – they patrol the woods. Though I suppose they might have spotted intruders and fired over their heads a couple of times.'

'I could have been mistaken – not about the shots but

their origin. It is difficult to tell where sounds come from at night. Perhaps they did come from the woods.'

'I'll have a word with the fellows if I remember.' I took this to mean Sir Ralph thought the matter of no consequence. I decided he was right and thought no more about it until later events made the incident assume a sinister significance.

# CHAPTER NINE

The hot weather returned. One afternoon I was strolling by the lake enjoying the pleasures of solitude; sometimes, in a house full of people one longs to escape.

I sat for a while on a bench overlooking the water where swans and moorhens were gliding about. I opened Goldsmith's *Poems* and began reading 'The Deserted Village'.

'You admire Goldsmith?' said a voice behind me. I turned round to find the hermit looking at me with a quizzical expression.

'Why, yes. Not as much as some others perhaps but—'

'Yes, he has his limitations. I too have been reading Goldsmith.'

'I noticed the book in your cell and found a copy in the library when I realized that some of the poems were unfamiliar to me. There is one, for instance, about a hermit. He looks very like you in the illustration – see!' I showed him.

'Ah, but I am unlikely to be approached by my lost love in male garb. These things happen only in fiction. Did you know Lady Denby was putting a hermit into her latest novel? She has asked me some very odd questions. I think she should have my assistance acknowledged on the title page: 'The Spanish Bandit' by a Lady and a Hermit.'

'That would sell more copies, I am sure.'

We continued talking for a while, entirely on the subject of literature. Then I stood up, saying I must return to the house to change for dinner.

'May I walk with you? We have to pass near my hermitage.'

'Of course. I enjoyed our conversation but aren't you supposed never to talk to people?'

'Silence and solitude suit me very well but sometimes I long for human speech – especially *intelligent* human speech.'

'Thank you!' Then I added, on impulse: 'Do you intend to spend the rest of your life like this? You have clearly enjoyed a much fuller existence.'

'Who can tell? At present I find the peace and quiet I need – "Far from the madding crowd's ignoble strife".'

I completed the verse:

'"Their sober wishes never learned to stray.

Along the cool sequestered vale of life

They kept the noiseless tenor of their way."'

'Ah yes,' he smiled gravely, 'one of my favourite poems.'

'And one of mine. Didn't General Wolfe say he'd rather have written Gray's Elegy than take Québec?'

'Yes – Wolfe.' He gave me a strange, searching look. 'He was fortunate to die as he did. The burden of command is very great.'

We walked a little further and came in sight of his dwelling. I felt there was some hidden meaning in his last remarks but could not fathom it.

'And here we are and I must bid you good evening. I see Colonel Hartley has sent me another bottle of wine so my dinner will be cheerful enough.'

He picked up the bottle which had been left just inside the entrance to his cave, bowed slightly and went into his cell, closing the door behind him.

That night was warm and I had difficulty falling asleep. I dozed fitfully for an hour or so and then lay tossing and turning and listening to the stable clock strike the hours. It was about two in the morning – about the same time as on a previous occasion – when I heard a shot fired: a single one this time.

I rose and went to the open window, listening intently. A few minutes later, another sound disturbed the silence – a splash as if something was being thrown into the lake. Bright moonlight flooded the landscape and once I thought I saw a shadowy figure running through the trees, but it was impossible to see any detail or even to decide whether it was male or female.

For a long time I stood watching and listening. Then weariness overcame me and I went back to bed and slept until morning.

I had always taken a short walk after breakfast, weather permitting, and I had brought up Sophie to do the same so we followed our usual habit and took a turn about the grounds. On this occasion our progress was interrupted in the most dramatic fashion. As we walked along one of the winding, tree-lined paths in the direction of the hermitage, we heard wild, frantic sobs before Elinor Denby burst into view, her bonnet tumbled from her head and her hair dishevelled. Her wide, staring eyes at once suggested she had just suffered some dreadful shock. She seemed relieved to see us.

'Oh, Miss Tyler!' She seized me by the arms, gripping so tightly I found it quite painful.

'He's dead!' she cried. 'The most horrible sight. Blood everywhere. Oh my God, what shall I do?'

'First try to calm yourself. Dear Elinor, you must try to tell us more clearly what you have seen.'

Between convulsive sobs she managed to stammer out a broken description of what had happened. She had noticed that the hermit's can of milk and a loaf of bread which were taken to him at seven every morning were still outside his door. Thinking he might be ill, she knocked, and receiving no reply, ventured to enter, where a shocking sight met her eyes.

'He's dead!' she repeated.

It was only afterwards I wondered what she was doing entering the hermit's cell on her own. Would it not have been more in order for her to have found one of the gardeners or returned to the house and despatched one of the servants to find out if there was anything wrong?

'Take her back indoors,' I said to Sophie, 'and I will go and see for myself. She may be mistaken.'

'I am not mistaken!' she cried furiously. 'And I am *not* going back to the house.'

'Very well, wait here. I shan't be long.'

I hurried to the hermitage and found, as she described, a can of milk and a loaf of bread placed near the door, which was ajar – left so by Elinor, I supposed.

I peeped inside, having tried to prepare myself for a

shocking sight. It was worse than I had imagined. The hermit lay sprawled on his bed still wearing his monkish robes. There was blood all over his pillow and a pistol in his left hand. There seemed little doubt he had shot himself. I drew back quickly, shaking at the knees and feeling decidedly queasy. It was necessary for me to regain my composure before rejoining the two girls but I longed to sit down with a glass of water and a kindly arm around me; whose arm I did not greatly care at that moment.

At last I managed to summon up enough self-possession to retrace my steps to where I had left Sophie and Elinor. The latter had mastered her hysteria but was still very distressed and I put my arm round her shoulders.

'Come along, my dear. We'll go back and find your father. He must be told at once and he'll know what to do.'

Sir Ralph and my brother were just leaving the stables dressed for riding but they both saw at once that something was wrong.

'What's the matter?' enquired Sir Ralph. 'Has Elinor had an accident?'

'No,' I said, answering for her. 'But she's had a dreadful experience. She found the hermit dead on his bed.'

'Dead? But I saw him yesterday and he looked perfectly well.'

'Not a natural death, I'm afraid. I think I'd better take Elinor indoors and give her sal volatile.'

'Never mind sal volatile. She needs a drop of brandy. Come now, my dear.' He patted her cheek with clumsy affection. 'You've had a nasty shock but you'll soon feel better. I'd better go and see for myself.'

George offered to go with him and I fancy Sir Ralph was

glad of his company.

'I want to be left alone,' said Elinor, as we made our way through a side door into the house. 'For heaven's sake don't let either of those two near me – you know who I mean.' It was obvious she was referring to Lady Denby and Mrs Thorpe. I reflected that I would certainly not want their cold comfort if I was distressed so I agreed soothingly and suggested she went straight up to her room and lie down for a while. I sent Sophie to find Elinor's maid and tell her to bring brandy, then I went upstairs with Elinor. She clung to the balustrade, as though she found great difficulty standing upright. As soon as she reached her room she ran to the bed, flung herself on top of it and gave way to wild tears. I began to suspect that this emotional outburst was not entirely the result of a disturbing experience. It was more like grief than shock.

I was reluctant to leave her in this state so I sat on the edge of her bed and waited quietly until the paroxysm subsided.

'No one understands,' she gulped at last, 'no one knows. I couldn't possibly tell anyone in this house – they are all so selfish and insensitive. Lady Denby thinks she's a martyr to sensibility but she wouldn't know what it was if it hit her in the face.'

'I'm inclined to agree.'

'Really?' She sat up, mopping her face with a sodden handkerchief. I found a towel, dipped it in her water jug and wiped her stained cheeks. I took away her handkerchief and gave her mine.

'Even dear Papa,' she continued, 'he doesn't understand. I couldn't possibly confide in him.'

'Doesn't it depend on what you have to confide?'

'I think I can trust you – I must tell someone – this is too much to bear alone.'

'Anything you tell me won't go further than this room,' I assured her.

'Have you ever loved anyone? I don't mean a brother or a father – I mean a man?'

'Oh, yes,' I twisted the ring on my finger, 'I was engaged to a young officer who was killed in Spain.'

'Then you know – you really understand?'

'Of course I do.' I tried not to push her too hard. The shock she had received that morning had broken open the shell she had built around herself.

'I loved him – oh, I did so love him. I think he loved me but he never said so. He was so kind, so gentle, so comforting. He was my only friend.' She gave way to sobs again and I waited patiently for her to recover.

We were interrupted briefly by Sophie at the door with the maid and a glass of brandy.

'Is she all right?' whispered Sophie, genuinely concerned.

'Not really, but I'm staying with her for the time being. If you can find out anything more, come up and tell me.'

I took the glass from Sophie and carried it over to the table at the side of the bed. When Elinor was sufficiently recovered I persuaded her to take a few sips.

I wondered how far this friendship with the hermit had progressed.

'You were close friends, then?' I suggested.

'Oh yes, we talked and talked. I lent him my books.'

'Goldsmith for one. It had a slip of paper in it.'

'Which I wrote. We met nearly every day if only for a few

minutes. He needed solitude yet I think he was lonely at times, as I was. He understood.'

'He never told you who he was?'

'No, and I respected his wish to keep his identity hidden. I thought he might eventually tell me. He must have been in utter despair to do such a dreadful thing – if only I had known – if only I could have helped.'

'Did he strike you as being very unhappy and depressed?'

'He was melancholic – very serious and inclined to look on the dark side of life – but then, so am I. Perhaps that is why we got on so well. I can't believe I'll never speak to him again.'

I appreciated the poor girl's wish to keep her friendship secret. I suggested she should spend the rest of the day in her room.

'You've had a dreadful experience; if you withdraw for a while no one will be surprised or require further explanation. You'll eventually find the courage to take part in everyday life again.'

I did not insult her by telling her she would get over it but when she asked me if it would always be an agony I said it would abate.

'At present it's like a sharp knife – in time the knife blunts. Grief comes in waves like the sea. In between the waves is a period of calm and the waves gradually come further and further apart. You will be able to bear it.'

'You have been very kind. No one else could understand. Thank you.'

It was a bizarre association, I reflected, between an 18-year-old girl and a man more than twice her age. Young girls are sometimes besotted by a mature man but not usually one as eccentric as Brother Caspar.

Sophie came up presently to report that the whole house was in uproar. A doctor had been sent for from Ashdale and Colonel Hartley, who was the local magistrate, was riding over from Shelbourne. Frank and Rowland seemed rather excited by the whole business and had gone outside but Lady Denby was making a great scene and calling for laudanum to calm her nerves.

'She's lying on the sofa, quite overcome,' she added, 'but I thought poor Elinor could do with some laudanum too so I've brought some. They seem to have plenty. No one's asked about Elinor.'

'That doesn't surprise me.'

I persuaded Elinor to swallow a small dose of the palliative, enough to calm her nerves and perhaps induce sleep. When she seemed more settled I sent for her maid to sit with her and then went downstairs. Before Sophie and I entered the morning room, we could hear Lady Denby's booming voice complaining loudly. On entering we found her lying on the sofa, draped in shawls and sipping a glass of brandy. Louisa Thorpe stood near the window, looking out over the park and obviously not listening to the lamentations of her friend.

Rowland and Frank were nowhere to be seen and George and Sir Ralph were still outside, presumably keeping watch over the scene of the tragedy until the doctor and Colonel Hartley arrived.

'How could he do this to me?' cried her ladyship. 'You'd have thought he owed me a certain amount of loyalty as I was the one who installed him at Lovegrove. No self-respecting hermit could have asked for more – two good meals a day – two good woollen robes, a comfortable cell and a convenient cave to shelter from rain and sun, a beautiful park to roam in and no *work* at all. What am I to do now? He was such a *refined* hermit and I suppose now I'll have to make do with some dirty old vagabond – if I can find anyone at all.

'It's too bad,' she continued, allowing no interruptions, 'he's showed no consideration at all. Totally selfish! The worst thing of all is that the shock has totally deprived me of the power to write. I doubt if my new novel will ever be finished.

'Then there's all the nastiness – the coroner nosing around and I'm told the corpse will be conveyed to the laundry when he has seen it. A corpse in the laundry – just imagine!' She shuddered. 'It doesn't bear thinking of. I do hope Colonel Hartley manages to hush it all up.'

'Elinor is staying in her room,' I said, when she had paused for breath. 'She has had a very bad shock.'

'*She's* had a bad shock? What do you suppose I've had? She hasn't had all the bother of hiring a hermit and getting him installed and maintained.'

'But she found the dead body,' Sophie interposed, 'that must have been horrid.'

'I did not ask for the opinion of an immature girl. Miss Tyler,' she looked at me for the first time, 'can you take her somewhere – I find her distracting.'

I took Sophie by the arm and led her out of the door.

'Distracting!' she exclaimed indignantly. 'That poor man is dead and all she can think of is her own inconvenience.'

'Let us get away as far as possible.'

'I wish that meant we were going home to Fairfield.'

'So do I but I fear we'll have to remain here until after the inquest.'

'When will that be?'

'Only the coroner can decide. He has to view the body and hear the opinion of the doctor.'

'Was it very horrid?'

'Pretty bad.' I opened the side door of the house and we stepped out into the fresh air.

# CHAPTER TEN

It was a relief to escape from overwrought emotions into the tranquil park. The morning was so bright, so warm and still that it was difficult to believe such a violent act had taken place in such beautiful surroundings. We followed our path to the lake, but on the side furthest from the hermitage.

'Look there – I think that's Colonel Hartley waving to us. I like him, don't you?' said Sophie.

'Yes, indeed.'

'I'm glad he is the magistrate. I thought Sir Ralph would be.'

'Colonel Hartley was the local magistrate before the Denbys came here – and his father before him. Yes, he wants to talk to us.'

The Colonel had begun walking towards us along the side of the lake so we set out to meet him. We met near one of the seats that overlooked the water.

'I very much wanted to see you,' he said. 'I hope neither of you is too distressed by what has happened.'

'Poor Elinor is dreadfully upset,' said Sophie, 'but then, she found the body. Then Aunt Charlotte went to have a look to make sure she'd not made some sort of mistake.'

He looked at me gravely. 'That must have been very shocking for you.'

'Not the worst shock I've ever had, but bad enough.'

'I think I may need your help, Miss Tyler. Sophie, do you think you could run back to the house and fetch your aunt's sketchpad and pencil?'

She needed no encouragement; glad to be of assistance she hurried off.

'How can I be of use?' I asked.

'I may need a helping hand – literally as I have only one of my own. I know I can rely on you to be absolutely discreet. Sir Ralph means well but he's a great fusspot and seems to have no idea how matters like this should be conducted. It was all I could do to stop him blundering round the cell, picking things up and moving them. He wanted to remove the body but I told him we must wait for the coroner.'

'I find it difficult to believe Brother Caspar shot himself a few hours after I had a pleasant conversation with him.'

'Indeed – tell me about it.'

I related the encounter of the previous afternoon.

'He seemed perfectly at his ease – quite good-humoured in fact and we walked back to the hermitage together. He saw you'd sent him a bottle of wine and he remarked he'd have a cheerful supper.'

'You saw the wine?'

'Oh yes – the bottle had been left just inside the entrance to the cave so that it was in the shade.'

'But I sent him no wine yesterday.'

'He certainly thought it was from you. Did anyone else ever send him any?'

'I think he'd have told me if they did.'

'I heard the shot at about two this morning just after the stable clock struck the hour.'

'Really?'

'And – this is odd – it was followed a few minutes later by a splash as though someone had thrown something into the lake.'

'Have you told anyone of this?'

'No. I heard two shots in the middle of the night about a week ago and I mentioned it to Sir Ralph, but he said it was probably the gamekeepers. He didn't seem very concerned.'

'Please say nothing to anyone about this. It may be important. There is something not right about the whole business. Like you, I find it difficult to believe this was a suicide but I have no proof it was anything else. Poor man – his was a tragic life and a tragic death, but not, I feel, self-inflicted.'

'You knew him well?'

'I don't think anyone knew him well. I shall, of course, make known his true identity which I could not do during his lifetime. He has kin in Devonshire who need to know and of course, the coroner must be informed.'

'And you know why he hid himself away from the world like this?'

He nodded. 'His real name was James Rushworth and eight years ago he was my colonel and I was a mere captain, both of us serving in the Peninsula. I need not go into the whole miserable business at this stage but he was held accountable for the escape of a French garrison. Everyone knew that he was not to blame. A certain general was mainly responsible. He had passed on the orders far too late and when they eventually arrived, Rushworth, I must admit, panicked a little. Lord Wellington thought we were much nearer to the fortress than was actually the case. He had a low opinion of the general, who had been foisted on him by the Horse Guards and was little more than a half-witted drunkard. Whether Wellington ever knew what had actually happened is debatable. Anyway, he criticized the regiment in his official despatch for allowing the garrison to escape. Rushworth was not mentioned by name but he took it as a personal affront. He asked for an inquiry but that was denied.

'Rushworth was not, I feel, of the right temperament to make a good soldier. He was immensely brave and did his duty with great devotion but he was too sensitive, too thin-skinned. He brooded and moped and even contemplated suicide.'

'*Then?*'

'Oh yes – though of course I was not told until long afterwards. Instead he sold his commission, quit the army and returned home. One of the majors was promoted colonel and two years later, after a few deaths, I gained the colonelcy of the regiment, which went on to redeem itself over and over again. The sad episode that had blighted Rushworth's career receded into the past but it still loomed large in his mind. The shame – or what he perceived as the shame of his disgrace – went with him. He chose to change his name and disappear. He wandered about the country, taking employment here and there: as a clerk, as a tutor, as a fencing master. . . .'

'But he had family in Devon?'

'An uncle who owns a large estate. Rushworth was his heir. Another man might have shrugged off the whole sad business and started again. Few people in England would know or understand or even care what had happened. Rushworth could not do that. He eventually saw the advertisement for a hermit, knew that I lived somewhere near and came to see me. I secured him the post, as you know.'

'He struck me as being very melancholic but yesterday evening he seemed perfectly serene.'

'I think his life here suited him. He had no decisions to make, no responsibilities, peace and quiet in pleasant surroundings and plenty of fresh air and good food. He seemed content and told me he was happier than he had ever been. That does not mean he was quite free of the depression that troubled him – it was something he had suffered all his life and was unlikely to disappear completely.

'When we're able to enter the cell after the coroner has seen the remains I would like you to make a sketch of the interior. There are also some questions I'd like to ask you, if you've no objection. I'm sorry to put you through this but I can hardly approach Miss Denby.'

'Of course not, I'm perfectly willing to help. I would like to be of use.'

Sophie arrived with my sketching materials. 'Here you are – please don't make me stay indoors. Lady Denby is still complaining and the whole house is in chaos. It's so gloomy in there and so peaceful out here, despite what has happened.'

'Yes, I'd rather you stayed with me,' I said, 'at least for the present. But first, I'd like you to go to the kitchen and ask the cook to prepare a picnic basket for us – and for Colonel Hartley, who will otherwise have to go hungry.'

'Not for the first time in my life,' he grinned.

'But not in England in peacetime, I hope. Sophie, I think

you'd better ask for a maid to bring the basket out to us here on this bench.'

'Do you think Lady Denby has turned against me?' said Sophie, hopefully. 'She was decidedly unpleasant.'

'No, I think that was a temporary fit of irritation. I'm sure she'll be gushing over you again very soon. You are important in her scheme of things.'

'Sophie and Rowland?' enquired Colonel Hartley when she had gone. 'I thought there was some such scheme in operation. I doubt if it will come to anything. I fancy Rowland will surprise us all before he is finished.'

'Really?'

But he said no more on the subject and we were interrupted by the Colonel's manservant, Sam Bates, who brought us the news that the doctor and the coroner had arrived together and required his presence. I liked the look of Sam Bates, who had served with the Colonel's regiment in the Peninsula and at Waterloo. He had a rough, open, weather-beaten face and a simple, direct manner. He was obviously someone to be trusted.

Colonel Hartley excused himself and I found myself alone for the first time that day; indeed, for the first time – the hours of sleep excepted – since I encountered Brother Caspar yesterday. It felt like an age ago and the horrors of the morning seemed quite unreal.

Sophie returned at last with a story to tell. 'The hamper will be sent,' she said. 'Cold ham and chicken, a little salad, a strawberry tart and a pot of cream. Oh, and spruce beer and lemonade.'

'Thank you – that sounds ideal for a hot day.'

'Everything is in uproar. The poor maid who takes the

hermit his food was in hysterics. "Such a nice gentleman!" she said. "treated me so kindly – spoke to me as though I was a lady!" Then she threw her apron over her head and refused to be comforted. So I thought it best to ask for something simple that wouldn't need much preparation.'

'That was very sensible of you.'

'Then I decided to get something to read from the library – we don't know how long we will be stuck out here. I overheard the most almighty row going on between Lady Denby and Mrs Thorpe. They were in the study next door and I could hear them shouting at each other, even through that heavy oak door. I got the impression that Mrs Thorpe was tired of Lady Denby's complaints and told her to shut up. Then her ladyship started telling her a few home truths. I distinctly heard her say: "You are a perfect disgrace and behaving like a common trollop!" Imagine! Now, if *I* shouted like that you'd tell me I was unladylike.'

'And so you would be. Lady Denby is a law unto herself and I strongly suspect Mrs Thorpe is not a lady.'

'Then I suppose she'll take herself off and Frank Lawrence with her, which would be a pity – he's amusing. Still, I suppose it will get her away from Papa, which is more important. On the other hand, you said we'd probably all have to stay here until after the inquest.'

'Inquests are usually held fairly promptly,' I told her. I reflected that a falling-out between Lady Denby and her old friend might, as Sophie supposed, lead to her early departure from Lovegrove. However, I did not trust her and felt sure that if this happened she would concoct some scheme for seeing my brother again.

# CHAPTER ELEVEN

After the remains of the supposed suicide were removed to the laundry, Colonel Hartley asked me to accompany him to the hermitage. Sophie, who was anxious to help, was given the task of drawing the outside of the cave.

We went inside. 'I hope this will not be a painful experience for you,' he said, 'and if you'd rather not do this, please say so.'

'No, I'm quite prepared.'

'Then tell me first, if anything has been disturbed in any way since you entered this morning and found the corpse.'

'I don't think so.' My eyes took in the bed, where the pillow had been covered with a cloth, and then I noticed the open box of pistols on the floor. One remained inside but the other was missing.

'Where—?' I began.

'Preserved as evidence. But the box was there when you entered? Sir Ralph started moving it away.'

'Yes, I'm sure that's where it was.'

'Then can you make a sketch of the room, exactly as it is?'

'I will try.'

'And another thing, if the recollection is not too

distressing, can you show in your sketch how the body was lying when you saw it? I will help you.'

I drew the room first, leaving blank the area where the body lay.

'It looked,' I said, 'as though he was seated on the side of the bed to shoot himself and then he fell backwards.'

'Quite so.' He moved behind me and watched me begin to sketch the dead man. Then he took the pencil from my hand.

'I've done some drawing myself in the past but you are so much better at it than I. Fortifications and battlefields are more in my line. Now – the pistol had fallen from his hand and lay here.' He made a swift sketch. 'Does that look right to you?'

We completed the picture between us, exchanging the pencil from time to time. I found it quite disturbing to find him standing so close with the front of his coat brushing against my back and his sleeve against my arm. There was an occasional, unavoidable contact of fingers.

'I think that will do very well,' he said at last, moving away. 'So we have a record of the scene as it was when you saw it this morning. Now, there are one or two other things which require your assistance. Could you pick up the pistol-box and put it on the table over here? Thank you – now close the lid.'

He produced a piece of cord from his pocket with two keys hanging from it.

'My friend Rushworth wore this round his neck. What with his beard and the cowl of his habit it would have been quite hidden. One key is to the trunk; the other, smaller one, to the pistol box. Let us try it in the lock.' He attempted to turn the key.

'As I thought, it doesn't fit. I can't say I ever observed the box very closely, but I felt sure this was different, and so it is.'

'But who would change the pistol box?'

'And the pistols. Whoever shot him.'

'You really think he was murdered?' There seemed to me a vast chasm between disbelieving someone had committed suicide and actually suspecting murder.

'Yes, and there's more than one reason, but not enough to achieve such a verdict at an inquest. I mentioned my suspicions to the coroner but he was rather dismissive.'

'But why do you suppose he was shot by someone else?'

'Firstly, my friend was right-handed yet the bullet entered the *left* temple and the pistol lay near his left hand. Secondly, he once told me he had attempted suicide but couldn't do it. He had placed the muzzle of the pistol in his mouth but could not bring himself to pull the trigger. That is the only sure way to do it. Let me show you.'

He opened the box, took out the remaining pistol, checked to make sure it was unloaded and then held it to his head. 'Quite heavy and awkward to hold steadily like this. The other way would be used by someone accustomed to firearms as he was.'

'But I can't understand why anyone would want to change the pistols.'

'For speed, simplicity and certainty. The cell was left open and there was no lock on the door. Anyone could have entered and examined the contents as I believe you did, unwillingly, with Rowland Webb. The murderer saw the pistols and then planned for his victim's apparent suicide. If he had used Rushworth's own pistols he would have had to unlock the box but he had no key and did not know where it was. If he had forced the lock it might have aroused suspicion. Besides, he would still have had to load the pistol by lantern, light which is not easy. I think he drugged the wine so that his victim was in a deep sleep but he still had to act quickly. It would have been much easier to buy *another* box of pistols, as much like the original as possible, load the gun in daylight at his leisure—'

'The shots I heard that Sir Ralph said were gamekeepers—'

'He was trying them out. Then he reloaded – came down here a few nights later in the early hours of the morning – found poor Rushworth unconscious – shot him through the head as he slept on his right side and arranged his body to look as though he had done the deed himself. Then he carried Rushworth's box to the lake and disposed of it. Now, I've noticed the absence of any wine bottle so I can only assume it was thrown away at the same time as the box.'

'But how could anyone be sure of finding a box of pistols similar to the ones the hermit owned?'

'Easy enough, I imagine. Many half-pay officers will have sold their pistols. I've no doubt they can be purchased at any gunsmith's. They are all much the same. Richer officers sometimes had various embellishments but most were perfectly plain. I never saw Rushworth's firearms – only the box and that was as nondescript as this one you see here. He had removed the brass plate with his initials; the same has been done to this box, you'll notice, but I'd swear the plate here was bigger.'

He sighed. 'I can't *prove* anything, of course. I've no doubt the verdict will be suicide and the poor fellow deserves better. This was a miserable, shabby way to die and the villain must be brought to justice somehow.'

'Do you think the murderer bought the pistols locally? If so, might it be worth visiting gunsmiths in neighbouring towns?'

'Indeed it might. That's a very good idea and well worth pursuing.'

I picked up the copy of Goldsmith's *Poems* which lay on the table and this time I looked inside the front cover. As I thought, it bore the name of Elinor Denby.

'Would it be in order for me to take this back to Elinor? It is her property and I can't see it has any bearing on what has happened.'

'Yes, I'm sure that's all right. You know, another thing has occurred to me. Most suicides leave letters to their family and friends – at the very least a scribbled note. I'm sure Rushworth was no exception.'

'There is one matter above all that I don't understand,' I said. 'I suppose anyone could come here to commit the crime, but why? What could possibly be the reason for killing so harmless a man? He hurt no one and he had nothing.'

'Even so, there could be a motive – there always is. Rushworth had a past – another life before he came here. Anyway, now we have done all we can in this place I must go and see what is happening in the laundry. I'll make sure the hermitage is guarded and Sir Ralph is arranging to have a chain and padlock fitted to the door.'

'Would it be worth looking in the trunk?' I asked.

'I was going to leave that until later, but as I have you here and you are willing to help. . . .'

The trunk held little of interest. There was a dressing-case containing shaving tackle – not that he needed any at Lovegrove – clothes, boots, brushes and combs. At any time he could have shaved off his beard, cut his hair and dressed normally. I suggested that he had not entirely given up the hope of returning to everyday life.

'That may be so,' said Colonel Hartley, 'but he never mentioned it to me.'

Matters became more interesting when we discovered a false bottom to the trunk, which, when lifted out, revealed a bundle of papers tied with tape and closely covered with writing. I handed them to the Colonel, who said, after a hasty glance, that they seemed to be a detailed account of Rushworth's part in the escape of the French garrison.

There was also a small watercolour of a handsome country house and a miniature of a dark-eyed young woman with a lock of hair in the back, several bundles of letters and documents, a leather wallet containing banknotes and a purse full of money including guineas.

'I wonder who the girl was?' I said.

'The love of his life, I believe. She married someone else while he was in Spain.'

I reflected that I would have waited years for Harry and at once dismissed the unknown woman as shallow and flighty. But of course, I did not know the circumstances.

'Here's his last will and testament,' I said, handing the document to my companion.

'Made about a year ago and witnessed by two of the gardeners. He leaves all his personal possessions to me – not that they amount to much – but he expresses the wish that I might eventually have printed the vindication of his conduct in the war.'

'You said he had an uncle.'

'Yes, in Devonshire. That little watercolour must be a picture of the house. He would have inherited everything eventually. I must write to the old man – even though the two hadn't met for years it will still be a shock.'

I collected all the items in the bottom of the trunk together and, having found the basket in which I had made my offering of fruit, put them neatly inside, covering every-thing with one of Brother Caspar's handkerchiefs.

'This will be easier to carry,' I said. 'I presume you don't want these things to be left here for others to find.'

'No, certainly not. You are remarkably thoughtful. I am glad you were here with me and not the coroner or Dr Stringer or the village constable – even Sam Bates. You understand.'

I thought he seemed moved; the calm, controlled demean-our cracked a little as he struggled to control emotion. 'Poor, unhappy soul!' he said. 'If he was going to die I wish to God it had happened in battle. This was unworthy of him.'

'At least he found peace here,' I said quietly after a pause, 'and I'm sure your friendship meant a great deal to him.'

'I hope so.' He seemed to master himself and gave me a quick smile. 'We must not waste time. There is one last thing I wanted to ask you. I would not presume to question Miss Denby concerning her discovery of the body. Anyway, I doubt if we could learn anything from it. I gather she is very distressed?'

'Greatly so but she seemed ready enough to confide in me. I was going to see her again as no one else seems to bother with her, so if you'd like me to talk to her—'

'If you don't mind. I find it strange that a young girl would enter a man's room like that. Are you sure she didn't know poor Rushworth a little better than her family supposed?'

'You have made an astute guess. She unburdened herself to me and I promised not to tell but as you've worked it out for yourself I must admit you are right. It was a friendship; no more than that, I am sure.'

'Of course, Rushworth would never have taken advantage of an innocent girl. See if you can find out if he had said anything that might indicate a threat to his life or if he saw some stranger in the park. Perhaps she noticed a particular depression of spirits or signs of anxiety – anything of that sort.'

I nodded and we left the cell.

Outside we found Sophie waiting impatiently and the village constable hovering discreetly at a distance, talking to Sam Bates.

'At last!' cried Sophie. 'I finished my sketch ages ago. Here.' She handed it to Colonel Hartley. 'It's not as good as Aunt Charlotte's, I'm sure, but at least you can tell what it's supposed to be.'

'It's excellent – just what's needed. Thank you, Miss Tyler Junior. It only needs Miss Tyler Senior to mark on it where the bottle of wine was found and it is all complete.'

I think he expected me to put a cross but I added a tiny drawing of a bottle. He laughed and thanked me and went off to the laundry to see what was going on.

Sophie watched him walk away. 'I think that when I *eventually* marry I'd like it to be someone like Colonel Hartley. Younger, of course, and with both arms.'

'I will keep a lookout for his double,' I promised her, 'though I doubt if we'll find it.'

'You were in the cell a very long time. What were you doing?'

'I made a sketch and we looked at the pistol box,'

'Ah, that must have been the locked box that puzzled me.'

'And we went through the hermit's trunk. Nothing of extraordinary interest – clothes, mainly, and bundles of papers which are in that basket that the Colonel gave to Sam Bates.'

'Is that all?' Sophie looked quizzical.

'What else could there be?'

She shrugged. 'I'm sure if I'd been shut in there with Rowland he'd have attempted to take liberties.'

'I've no doubt he would and I trust you'd give him no such opportunity. But then, Colonel Hartley is a gentleman and I'm afraid Rowland, for all his swagger, is not.'

As we made our way back to our bench I told Sophie I intended to visit Elinor again before dinner.

'Would you like me to come with you?'

'No, I think it would be better if I saw her alone. She's more inclined to confide in me if no one else is there, I'm sure you understand.'

Sophie nodded. 'She's such a strange girl, I'm still not sure if I like her or not. I feel sorry for her having to put up with that awful stepmother and her horrid friend. Sir Ralph is pleasant enough but he doesn't do anything to help.'

'Ah, that brings me to the question I was going to ask you. What would you say to asking Elinor to come back to stay with us for a few weeks? I'm sure it would do her the world of good and I think she'd open out a little in sympathetic company. We might even be able to do something about her clothes and hair.'

'I think that's a lovely idea,' said Sophie generously.

'You are a dear, good girl and you deserve the best husband in the world!'

Later in the day, I went, as promised, to see Elinor, who looked quite dreadful, with red, swollen eyes. She was surrounded by crumpled handkerchiefs and her hair hung in damp strands round her tear-stained face. She had slept, however, and still seemed slightly dazed, but at least she was not sobbing and spoke coherently.

I talked to her for a long time, dropping questions in randomly so that it would not appear like an interrogation. At the end I knew little more. She could tell me only that Brother Caspar had never mentioned having any enemies and had seemed no more depressed when she last saw him than at any other time. As for strangers . . .

'Well,' she said, uncertainly, 'I did see a strange woman, rather fashionably dressed in a vulgar sort of way. I don't think it was anything to do with Caspar. *He* saw her and asked me if I knew who she was but I didn't recognize her. Anyway, I didn't see her face properly though she seemed quite young.'

'When was this?'

'About a fortnight ago.'

'I suppose it could have been someone coming to see one of the servants.'

'That's what I thought, but – she looked troubled.'

'Has it anything to do with what happened at the Unicorn? You went back for your reticule and when you returned I thought you'd had a shock.'

'I had – but I can't tell you at present. It will all come out eventually but I really can't cope with any more today.'

'Then let's leave it for now. Here's that Goldsmith you lent to Brother Caspar; I thought you'd like to have it back. It was lying on his table.'

She clutched it to her bosom like some precious relic and shed a few tears. When she was quieter I revealed my plan for taking her back with us to Fairfield.

She was transformed. 'Oh yes, that would be so lovely! Are you sure I'd be welcome?'

'Of course you would! Sophie would be glad to have a companion of her own age.' I thought this slight exaggeration was permissible in the circumstances. 'I have yet to ask my brother,' I continued, 'but if Sophie and I wanted to invite Napoleon Bonaparte for a stay he'd be quite agreeable. We must ask your father too, of course, but I'm sure he'll consent.'

'Oh yes, and the others will be glad to get rid of me.'

'I think you may need a change of scene. This house is rather gloomy for someone in low spirits.'

'It isn't the house, it's the people.'

'I think I know what you mean. Have courage, this is the very worst. At least you'll find a pleasanter atmosphere at Fairfield.'

'I know I shall, if you can put up with me.'

'You must not have such a low opinion of yourself. Sophie and I only want you to be our friend and my brother is the kindest man in the world.'

She began crying again.

# CHAPTER TWELVE

The atmosphere in the house at dinner was unpleasantly tense; with a corpse in the laundry and an inquest pending, it could scarcely be anything else. Amelia Denby and Louisa Thorpe seemed to have made up their quarrel and appeared particularly – indeed, nauseatingly – affectionate and gushing. It was 'dearest Louisa' and 'kindest Amelia'.

George was unusually quiet and gloomy. I had not expected him to be so affected by the tragedy but I soon discovered that his silence and melancholy rose from quite another reason. Elinor was not present, which did not surprise me, and Rowland was also missing but Frank Lawrence had turned up and was trying to improve the air of dejection that engulfed the table.

'A good ride or a walk in the fresh air is the best thing in the world for raising the spirits,' he declared. 'I went as far as Ashdale and back and had something to eat at the Unicorn at about one. I saw Rowland in the town; I think he had the same idea. After all, there was nothing we could do to help.'

'*Some* people made themselves useful by all accounts,' said Louisa Thorpe vindictively, looking in my direction.

'Miss Tyler has been helping Colonel Hartley search the hermit's cell. What else she helped him with I don't know.'

I said nothing, fearful of an angry outburst that I would regret later.

'He asked my sister to help because she can be relied on,' said George, 'which is more than can be said for most women.'

'Extraordinary!' boomed Lady Denby. 'The whole sex is condemned out of hand. Really, Cousin George, I must say that either you exaggerate or your personal experience has been unfortunate.'

'You could say that,' murmured George, reddening slightly.

'This conversation is galloping towards a precipice,' said Frank cheerfully. 'Let's try a different horse. Where's Elinor?'

'In her room,' said Sir Ralph. 'The poor girl's nerves are quite shattered. It was she who discovered the body after all.'

'Yes,' said his wife with a puzzled expression, 'we still don't know how that came about. What was she doing entering my hermit's cell?'

'She saw he hadn't touched his bread and milk and thought he might be ill,' said Sir Ralph.

'Then it was a most improper course of action,' declared Lady Denby. 'Heaven knows what she might have found.'

'I should think finding someone shot through the head is bad enough,' I said.

Lady Denby ignored me. 'Why didn't she go back to the house and send one of the menservants to investigate?'

'She acted on impulse,' I said. 'Girls of her age do. She was concerned.'

'I don't see why she should be,' her ladyship remained unconvinced. 'What was the hermit to her?'

That proved a little too close for comfort but Sir Ralph defended his daughter. 'She's a kind-hearted girl,' he said. 'You don't always give her credit for her good qualities.'

In the drawing-room the atmosphere was no better. When the gentlemen joined us I saw Louisa Thorpe pointedly draw aside her skirts to indicate to George that he was to sit beside her on the sofa. Instead he sat down by me.

'What's the matter?' I asked. 'I thought you enjoyed Mrs Thorpe's company.'

'Not any more,' he muttered. 'I was never so deceived about anyone in my life.'

'I tried to warn you,' I said softly, 'but you wouldn't listen.'

'I wish I had. You always had plenty of good sense, Charlotte.'

'But what has happened to make you change your mind?'

'I can't tell you – at least not yet. But that woman is utterly depraved. She disgusts me. I can hardly bear to be in the same room with her. We must go home as soon as possible.'

Although I was glad to hear it, I knew I would not leave Lovegrove without a pang of regret.

'George,' I said, 'would you mind greatly if Elinor came home with us? Sophie is quite happy to have her company for a few weeks.'

'Elinor?' He sounded as though he was trying to remember who she was. 'A quiet, plain girl. No, she'd be no bother. Whatever you please. Better ask her father. Don't suppose her stepmother cares what happens to her.'

'That was the impression I got. Elinor had a dreadful

shock this morning and needs a change of scene. These are not the best surroundings for a sensitive girl.'

'Indeed they are not. I'll be glad to get Sophie away. I'm never going to bring her here again – at least, not while that woman is visiting.'

I was about to get up in order to ask Sir Ralph's permission to invite Elinor to Fairfield when George caught me by the arm and pulled me back down again.

'Don't leave me,' he hissed. 'If you move from here that woman will take your place – she keeps trying to catch my eye, confound her.'

'So she obviously doesn't know why you have changed your mind about her. Did you see or hear something?'

'Yes – I'll tell you later. You ought to know, though it's scarcely fit for a lady's ears.'

I was extremely intrigued and began to make wild conjectures but George had obviously witnessed some incident that he could tell me about only in absolute privacy.

Towards nine o'clock Rowland arrived, still in riding clothes. He said he had already dined at the Unicorn.

'It's all over the town, you know – all sorts of mad rumours flying about.'

'What sort of rumours?' enquired Lady Denby.

'Oh – Sir Ralph shot the hermit thinking he was a poacher; the hermit got shot when he tried to intervene in a duel – I can't imagine who they thought had been fighting one – and most idiotic of all, he'd been shot by a jealous mistress.'

'I hope you did your best to counteract such pernicious nonsense,' said his mother.

'They'll find out soon enough when the results of the inquest are published.'

*

The inquest was a disagreeable experience which I did my best to forget afterwards, so my recollections remained hazy. It was held in the Assembly Room at the Unicorn, which was not used in summer and had a stale and shabby atmosphere. I was aware from the first of an antagonism between the coroner and Colonel Hartley. It was decidedly one-sided but I could not help wondering if the former – a fussy, pedantic, self-important attorney – might be jealous of the local military hero with his air of quiet authority and his clear, concise manner of speaking. Coroner Bailey was, after all, no more than a provincial lawyer with a limited knowledge of the greater world. He was quick to dismiss the Colonel's opinions as prejudiced because he had been a friend of the deceased.

Colonel Hartley gave evidence of the hermit's true identify, emphasizing his brave conduct in the army and explaining that 'some unfortunate experiences in Spain' had induced him to give up his military career and pursue a humble civilian life under another name, eventually withdrawing from the world in his role as hermit at Lovegrove. He said he had communicated news of James Rushworth's death to his closest relative, an uncle who owned a considerable property in Devonshire.

He then produced our sketch, pointing out how awkward it would have been for a right-handed man to shoot himself in such a fashion but the coroner gave it only a cursory glance. 'You showed me this before – it proves nothing.'

The Colonel had to concede, when questioned, that the dead man had been of a melancholy disposition though he qualified that by saying he had been more tranquil of late. Then, when pressed further, he was forced to admit that

James Rushworth had told him of a previous attempt at shooting himself.

The fact that the eventual deed had been carried out by the left hand rather than the right, and in a different manner from that originally attempted, was dismissed as of no importance. Colonel Hartley could have been mistaken; he could not *prove* the man was right-handed and some people can use the left hand as easily as the right.

I was obliged to give evidence as I had discovered the body. Elinor had been passed over as unfit to appear and unable to describe what she saw as she only caught the merest glimpse of the tragic scene.

I was asked if I knew the deceased and I stated that I had had two short conversations with him, the latter of which was on the evening before his death. I pointed out that he had seemed quite cheerful on that occasion and was looking forward to a bottle of wine with his supper – a gift of unknown origin, it appeared later.

This seemed to make no impression at all. The local tradesmen on the jury looked glum and restless and were obviously eager to get back to their daily occupations.

'Why would anyone wish to shoot this man when no one even knew his identity?' demanded the coroner, who rapidly guided the jury towards the conclusion he desired. They wasted no time in bringing in a verdict of suicide.

The funeral followed, which of course could not be a religious one, nor could the hermit be buried in consecrated ground. Colonel Hartley paid for an expensive coffin and planned to remove the deceased to his own estate and bury him in the grounds but Lady Denby objected strongly.

'He is *my* hermit; this is where he lived; this is where he died and this is where he should be buried.'

She then suggested an idea that was so appropriate that everyone, even the Colonel, agreed that it was the best course to follow.

'The nave of the old priory church has a crypt beneath. If the poor man was buried there he would be in consecrated ground.'

Some of the flagstones in the nave were duly removed so that the coffin could be lowered into the dank underground chamber. Lady Denby ignored the tradition that ladies do not attend funerals by declaring that this was not a real funeral as no clergy were present and the Prayer Book could not be used. She decided that there ought to be some sort of ceremony, which she interpreted as a flowery oration composed by herself, accompanied by a scattering of rose petals flung with a dramatic gesture into the open grave.

Colonel Hartley stood at a distance, head bowed. I took up a position in the shadow of an archway, making myself as inconspicuous as possible. As I was the last person – with the exception of the murderer – to see the hermit alive and one of the first to find him dead I thought I should be there. At the back of my mind was a stronger feeling that I wished to support Colonel Hartley.

Lady Denby led Sir Ralph and the other men of the party back to the house but the Colonel stayed behind. He approached the grave and watched as two of the gardeners replaced the flagstones. Waiting until he was alone, apart from Sam Bates, who stood at a discreet distance, I slipped out of the shadows and went to his side. He looked surprised but then smiled.

'Thank goodness it's you,' he said, 'and not Lady Denby

with her histrionics.'

'It would have been funny if it wasn't so desperately sad.'

'He deserved better. I'm determined to find out who killed him and bring the guilty one to justice. That's why I insisted on paying for a good coffin. One day he'll be removed to a proper grave in a churchyard and have a real funeral.' He brought out of his pocket a worn and tattered copy of the *Book of Common Prayer*.

'Chaplains were often in short supply when we were campaigning. It was sometimes my duty to read part of the burial service over the graves of some poor fellows. I thought I'd do that now, if you'd like to stay.'

I think it was one of the most moving experiences of my life. When he had finished I could not speak.

'There is no more to be done,' he said, putting his book away. 'I must go.' He turned to me, saw my distress and put his hand on my shoulder.

'Are you all right?'

I nodded, longing for him to put his arm round me but he let me go.

'I'll walk with you back to the house,' he said.

'There's no need – I can see someone who may need my company,' I said, my voice unsteady. I had observed a small, huddled figure sitting with her back to the wall and her knees drawn up like a statue of grief on a monument.

'Ah, Miss Denby, poor girl! Yes, you must go to her. I will see you again soon, I hope, before you go home. Goodbye.'

His last words struck a chill but I had more immediate concerns. I was about to ask Elinor what she was doing there and then realized it was a foolish question. She was red-eyed with weeping.

'You'll think I do nothing but cry,' she gulped, 'but I had to be here. My stepmother made a fool of herself as usual but Colonel Hartley – he did exactly the right thing. It meant more than a church funeral. It's what my friend would have wanted.'

'Of course, you know now who he was.' It occurred to me that the little she had heard of Rushworth's background would give him an additional air of romance and gallantry.

'Yes, and I mean to find out more. I'm ready to go back now. Do you mind if I walk with you?'

That evening Elinor appeared at dinner for the first time since before the shooting.

'Well, look who's here!' cried Rowland. 'The return of the prodigal.'

'I haven't been wasting my substance in riotous living,' she retorted waspishly, 'unlike some I could mention. And I don't like veal.'

'Veal?' Rowland looked bewildered.

'Fatted calf,' I murmured.

'Oh *that*! No, I suppose weak gruel is more in your line.'

'Take it easy, Rowland,' Sir Ralph admonished him, 'the poor girl's had a bad time.'

'More than you can imagine,' said Rowland.

'What does that mean?' demanded Lady Denby.

'Oh, nothing in particular. I thought she was making heavy weather of the whole thing. Anyone would think she was a sorrowing widow instead of just having a shock at discovering a suicide.'

That was a little too near the truth to be comfortable and the remark was not lost on Elinor, but no one else seemed to take it for more than its face value.

'What she experienced was quite bad enough,' said Sir Ralph, 'especially for a girl with delicate nerves.'

'*She* has nerves!' cried Lady Denby. 'What about *my* nerves, pray? I haven't been able to write a word since this dreadful thing happened. If you have any sense, Elinor, you will return to everyday life and keep yourself occupied. You haven't touched the piano for days. You must play for us this evening. You really are quite a competent pianist and you must keep in practice or you will lose your ability.'

Elinor did indeed play for us that evening but not before I heard a brief exchange in undertones between Rowland and her.

'You go too far,' she hissed. 'Take care what you say or you'll regret it.'

'So would you!'

'Would I? I don't really care any more and I'm leaving here soon anyway.'

Rowland looked decidedly uneasy.

'D'you think she'll be fit to travel if we leave the day after tomorrow?' whispered George, who as usual, now, was sitting beside me on the sofa. I still had no idea why he had broken off with Mrs Thorpe. On the only occasion I had been able to speak to him alone he said he didn't wish to talk about it as the subject was too painful, and he was having second thoughts about telling me something so disgusting. Naturally I was even more curious.

'I'm sure Elinor is longing to escape from here,' I said. 'Sophie wants to go home and I know you are desperate to get away.'

'So are you, I'm sure.'

I did not answer. True, I longed to leave Lovegrove and its unattractive residents but there was one person I feared I might never see again. George noticed my reluctance.

'Don't tell me you like it here? It was all very fine at first but things have not turned out well and there is no longer anything to keep us.'

'True,' I said, 'we really must go.'

Elinor had been playing some rather slow, melancholy piece. It sounded like something from a requiem mass.

'Oh, *do* play something more cheerful, Elinor,' cried Lady Denby, interrupting her performance. 'That's far too gloomy. You are making us all depressed – yourself included. Find something light and cheerful to entertain us.'

'You'll find some of my French songs there,' suggested Louisa Thorpe, 'and if you play one or two of those and I sing, I guarantee I can lift everyone's spirits.'

In response Elinor slammed the piano shut and ran from the room.

'Well, really!' exclaimed Lady Denby. 'What can have provoked that outburst?'

'That girl has a temper – it needs dealing with,' observed Mrs Thorpe.

'Double double, toil and trouble,' muttered George. 'What a pair of witches! I feel sorry for that poor girl. She'll be better off with us.'

But matters took an unexpected turn. Next morning Elinor was missing.

# CHAPTER THIRTEEN

It was Elinor's maid who reported that her mistress was not in her room when she went to wake her in the morning. As her bed had been slept in, it was concluded that she had gone out very early. She had not taken anything with her in the way of luggage but, judging from clothes that were missing, had just put on a dress, bonnet, and shawl as she would for any day's outing.

'No, the young lady wasn't carrying anything,' said one of the gardeners who had seen her leave, 'only one of those little reticule things. I thought it was strange as it was early so I went over and asked if there was anything I could help her with. "No, thank you," she said, "I'm just going out for a few hours!"'

A similar report was given by the lodge-keeper who found the bell being rung at half past six by Miss Denby wanting the gate opened. He had also found it odd that the young lady was going out on her own at such an hour but 'the gentry sometimes did eccentric things.'

'Idiots!' cried Lady Denby. 'Why didn't they stop her or at least come straight to us and tell us?'

The house was soon in uproar. Sir Ralph sent two

menservants out to look for his errant daughter and then, on a hint that she had started to walk to Ashdale and had then been picked up by the carrier's cart, he drove out in the same direction in the gig.

All was to no avail. On reaching the town Elinor seemed to have vanished. It was market day and the streets were crowded. She was a small, inconspicuous figure, plainly dressed, and no one remembered having seen her. I might perhaps have provided a sketch but Sir Ralph took off in a great hurry despite his wife's assurances that Elinor would be perfectly all right and if she wasn't she would have brought it on herself. Sir Ralph, however, was haunted by all the imagined horrors that could befall an innocent girl in an English country town on market day.

I was anxious about Elinor but not greatly perturbed. I was more concerned about her state of mind than about the possibilities of abduction, assault and murder. Several more servants were despatched after Sir Ralph to help him in his search and the house was left in chaos. The family and guests were dispersed, most of them trying to avoid Lady Denby. Luncheon consisted of a cold collation set out in the dining room for everyone to help himself. It was then I saw George.

'Where have you been?' I asked. 'I've looked everywhere for you. What are we to do about leaving tomorrow if Elinor has disappeared? We can't very well go without her.'

'I know,' he said gloomily, 'I've sent someone into Ashdale to cancel the post-chaise. I sometimes think we are doomed to stay on here.'

'Doomed?' cried a throaty female voice. 'Oh come, Mr Tyler, surely it isn't as bad as that.'

He scarcely suppressed a groan.

'Anyone would think you've been avoiding me,' she continued, tapping him playfully on the shoulder with her fan. 'I'm sure you don't want to escape from *me*!'

She sat down beside him and at once he pushed his plate away, excused himself and left the room.

'Whatever is the matter with your brother?' she asked me. 'He's been trying to avoid me for the last few days. I don't know what I've said or done to upset him.'

'Neither do I,' I told her. 'Whatever it is, he hasn't confided in me.'

'So there *is* something. I thought so! I must have a word with him privately.'

'Are you sure that would be wise? George can be very stubborn at times. Once he has made up his mind nothing can make him budge.'

'I can but try. I can usually cajole any man out of a fit of the sulks and I'm sure that's all it is. But are you all determined on leaving tomorrow?'

'That is certainly what we planned but Elinor's disappearance has made our arrangements very uncertain. We have postponed our departure.'

She seemed delighted. 'Oh, I am so glad. This house will seem so lifeless without you all, especially since this disagreeable business of the suicide – to say nothing of that silly girl's behaviour. What can she be thinking of?'

'She is very unhappy.'

'Really? I can't think why; a lovely ancient house to live in, a rich indulgent father, a literary genius for a stepmother – what more could she possibly want?'

'Some affection and consideration perhaps.'

'I'd have said she was overindulged but then, I am probably a better judge of character than you as I've had more experience of life.'

'Of course,' I said, 'you have known the tragedy of losing a dearly loved husband.'

She gave me a hard look. It was no secret that Mr Thorpe had been a mean-spirited, tight-fisted old man and the marriage had not been happy.

'Ah, poor Thorpe!' she sighed, deciding to take my remark at face value. 'And I am reduced to life in a cottage after being the mistress of a fine house.'

'There you are, Louisa!' Lady Denby sailed into the room like a ship with pennons streaming. 'Everyone seems to have disappeared. I'm becoming so concerned about Sir Ralph. He went charging off in such an agitated state. The doctor has warned him about this sort of thing but he won't listen. I'm sure we should have heard something by now. And where is Rowland? He's never here when I want him.'

'I expect he's gone off in search of Elinor,' I said.

'I can't think why – there are plenty of other people to do that. Whose plate is that?' She surveyed George's untouched luncheon.

'My brother's. I don't know where he went.'

'I frightened him away,' cried Louisa gaily.

'It must've been something fearsome for him to leave his food,' observed her friend. 'He must be hungry. I certainly am – at least, I would be if I wasn't so beset by anxiety. I doubt if I can manage more than a couple of mouthfuls.'

I watched as she helped herself to several thick slices of ham and cold beef and a large portion of pork pie. The dining-room clock chimed one. Elinor had been gone for six and a half hours.

An hour later Sir Ralph returned looking ashen-faced and decidedly ill. He declared his search had proved fruitless. 'I couldn't go on,' he admitted. 'I've had such pains.'

'Pains?' cried Lady Denby. 'Where are the pains?'

He confessed that they were in the region of his heart, at which his wife insisted that he should go to bed immediately – helped by two of the remaining servants. She then sent an urgent message to Dr Stringer.

'I'll be all right,' he groaned, 'if only Elinor would come back.'

'If and when she does I'll give her a dressing-down she'll never forget. That wicked girl! She is responsible for this! She could kill her own father with her stupid, selfish behaviour!'

Sir Ralph did not seem greatly cheered by this last observation but was quite willing to be put to bed to await the arrival of the doctor.

George, I discovered, had joined the flight to Ashdale ostensibly to help with the search for the missing girl, but also to escape the clutches of Mrs Thorpe and enjoy a steak at the Unicorn.

My only thought was to avoid the 'pair of witches' so I took myself out of doors to the front of the house so that I could watch for any arrivals. I took my sketchbook and watercolours and began to work on a painting of the priory ruins. Sophie followed me but then grew bored, complained of the heat and returned indoors, where, I heard later, she had gone up to explore the collection in the gallery with Frank Lawrence. Apparently they had spent an hilarious time opening cabinets and playing with the exhibits and trying on bits of armour. I was rather concerned when I heard about it but Sophie assured me he had behaved very correctly. 'He's a great deal more fun than Rowland – he says the cleverest things!'

I reflected that it probably mattered little as we were soon to leave.

Back in the park I saw the doctor arrive and, about twenty minutes later, Colonel Hartley, accompanied by his manservant, Sam Bates. I at once hastened to tell them of the latest developments. The Colonel seemed concerned about Sir Ralph's alarming symptoms.

'Driving about in this heat consumed by anxiety is enough to try someone younger and less portly than Sir Ralph. I hope it doesn't prove to be anything immediately dangerous.'

'The doctor arrived a few minutes ago so we're hoping for the best.'

'I was expecting Sir Ralph to join us this afternoon. He gave us permission to conduct a little experiment. Come and watch.'

We walked around the house to the lake, where two men were already waiting in a boat.

'Now we're here and all prepared we may as well go ahead.' The Colonel led the way to the end of the path from the hermitage. Then he signalled to the boat to come nearer.

'Now, Bates, from here throw as far as you can.'

I had noticed Sam Bates was carrying a crude wooden box under his arm. He hurled it into the water, where it fell with a heavy splash.

'Just the weight of a box of pistols. The water here is fairly shallow – it shelves down in a slope. I reckon it's no more than five feet deep where the box fell. If anything else is there it may be possible to find it.'

The boat came nearer and the men spent the next half hour with poles and nets, stirring up a great deal of mud. They fished out several bottles, an unrecognizable lump of metal, a bucket with no base and part of a broken hay-fork. Then they gave a shout of triumph.

'I think that may be it!' cried the Colonel. It was indeed the missing pistol box. Bates resourcefully produced a bit of old towel and dried it carefully. There it was, the battered mahogany box with the missing initial plate that I had seen in the hermit's cell that day Sophie, Rowland and I had invaded his privacy. It was very like the replacement present when the body was discovered.

The Colonel produced the key and turned it in the lock. 'It still works – but then, it hasn't been in the water very long.'

Inside lay two officer's pistols with all the usual accoutrements of powder flask, ramrod and various tools.

'So now we know for sure,' said Colonel Hartley, 'I'm sending Bates here on a tour of gunsmiths' shops armed with your sketches.'

'Surely you don't think anyone from the house was responsible?'

'We don't know, but we can at least eliminate any possible suspects.'

'Like Lady Denby,' I suggested, scarcely suppressing a giggle. 'I can just imagine her in turban and flowing shawls creeping about in the night intent on felony.'

He laughed. 'I think we can safely omit her from any investigations. But I am very pleased about our discovery this afternoon. I hardly dared hope we'd find anything. This is still no real proof in a court of law. Someone might suggest that poor Rushworth had two sets of pistols and threw one away for some reason. We can't prove there was a substitution, not unless Bates unearths something significant.'

'I'll do my best, sir.'

'When have you ever done anything else?'

The Colonel paid the two Lovegrove retainers for their help – a task they seemed to have enjoyed – and the box was wrapped in a piece of sacking and given to Bates to take back to Shelbourne.

'Go without me,' he told the man. 'I must call at the house and see how Sir Ralph is faring.'

We returned to the house together and entered by a side door. The doctor was just leaving, having bled Sir Ralph and administered a sleeping draught. Lady Denby was hovering over him, refusing to believe her husband was not near death.

'I assure your ladyship that Sir Ralph is sleeping peacefully, as you have seen for yourself,' Dr Stringer assured her. 'His valet is sitting with him and there is no need for you to be there also. I see no cause for alarm if he is allowed to rest for a few days. Keep him on a light diet – no alcohol until I say so – and make sure he is free from anxiety as far as possible.'

'That is highly unlikely at present.'

'Well, don't tell him anything alarming if you can help it. With any luck he'll stay unconscious until morning, when I'll call again. I'm afraid I must go now. Don't despair, he's very robust for his age. It's a common enough complaint with men of his constitution.'

The doctor departed, pleading another patient in need of a visit.

Colonel Hartley paid his compliments, adding sympathy for all the troubles Lady Denby was undergoing that day, and then took his leave. He told her nothing of what had transpired that afternoon at the lake. I had an idea she would consider it a great deal of nonsense and a waste of time. I needed little persuasion to accompany the Colonel back to the gate. He collected his horse from the stables and walked beside me with the reins over his arm. We had not gone very far when we saw a carriage coming towards us. The occupants were Rowland, Elinor and a strange young woman with a baby in her arms. My brother rode alongside. All looked exceedingly grim except the stranger, who looked frightened.

# CHAPTER FOURTEEN

The confrontation took place in the Great Hall. I had parted from Colonel Hartley, promising to inform him of the outcome of this new development, and made my way back to the house. As usual, the rest of the party – or what was left of it – had assembled before dinner. The moment the doctor had left, Lady Denby went up to lament over Sir Ralph. As he was blissfully unaware of her presence and his valet sat in attendance, she declared she could not bear to see her beloved spouse in such a woeful state. She hastily changed for dinner and came down to minister to her guests: Mrs Thorpe, Frank Lawrence, Sophie and me. I had no time to change unless I was willing to miss what promised to be an exciting scene.

The prodigals all entered at the same time, the two women first and then Rowland and George. The latter sidled over to me for protection in case Mrs Thorpe staged a flank attack.

Lady Denby stared at the incomers like an avenging Fury. 'What has been going on?' she demanded. 'Elinor, you owe us all an explanation. You've almost driven your poor father into his grave with your reckless behaviour. He's lying in his bed now at death's door.'

'Papa is ill? I must go to him!'

'You'll do no such thing! No one is allowed to see him. He must rest. And what are you doing, Rowland? Was it you who found her?'

'Not exactly.' He looked sheepish. 'I suppose you could say she found me.'

'And this young woman – who is she?'

'His wife!' Before Rowland could answer, the newcomer spoke for herself. She was a handsome girl, no more than twenty or so with copious chestnut hair, pink cheeks and shining hazel eyes. She was smartly dressed in a rather showy style: a canary yellow pelisse and an over-decorated bonnet. The child in her arms whimpered.

A deathly silence was broken by a hoarse, choking enquiry.

'His wife?' repeated Lady Denby. 'What do you mean by that, pray?'

The young woman, who had looked nervous when she first entered, had gained confidence and viewed her ladyship with a defiant air.

'Rowland and I were married nine months ago in Peckham. This is your little granddaughter, Arabella.' The voice had a strong Cockney accent and would, I felt sure, become shrill under pressure of emotion.

'Rowland – explain!'

'Well,' he shifted from one foot to the other uneasily, 'I met Carrie about a year ago and – er—'

'We fell in love!' Carrie finished the sentence for him.

'And how did you meet, pray?' enquired Lady Denby.

'My father kept the Bull Inn and Rowland used to come there with his cronies to play cards and drink.'

Lady Denby passed her hand over her brow as though about to faint. Mrs Thorpe proferred her smelling salts but her ladyship declined them with a gesture.

'So you are a publican's daughter?'

'That's right. It's a very respectable place – quite large and well appointed.'

Lady Denby had been doing a calculation. 'That child can't be less than three months old and you say you were married nine months ago? You fool, Rowland, why did you have to marry her? Sir Ralph and I would have dealt with the matter if you'd confided in us.'

'Oh, he had to marry me,' said Carrie brazenly, 'Pa insisted and he can get very nasty if thwarted. He has friends who know how to look after his best interests. But don't you want to look at your grandchild?'

'I certainly do not. There must be some way out. This marriage can't be legal.'

'I'm afraid it is,' admitted Rowland, 'I'm of age, after all.'

'It was a proper wedding in church and we signed the register and everything and there were plenty of witnesses.' Carrie was beginning to sound indignant. Now facing her towering, raging mother-in-law she had found her voice. Rowland was quite subdued. I reflected that in this marriage it was clear who would be the dominant partner.

'I think you might at least ask me to sit down as I'm carrying the baby,' Carrie complained.

'Yes, sit down, my dear,' said Rowland. 'Mama's had a shock. I told you she'd be angry but she'll come round when she gets to know little Arabella.'

Carrie sank into a chair with a shake of her ostrich plumes.

'I have no desire to get to know little Arabella. This is all too much. And what has all this to do with you, Elinor? Did you know about this marriage?'

'Not at first. I found out that day we went to the Unicorn for luncheon. I met Rowland coming out of one of the rooms when he was supposed to be miles away. This young woman was standing in the doorway with her child. I saw him kiss them both. He then saw me looking at them – the girl went back inside but he couldn't ignore me. He admitted then that he was married but made me promise not to tell anyone. He said he wanted to introduce the idea to his mother gradually.'

'Gradually? How could anything like this be gradual? It was always going to be a shock.'

'He knew about my friendship with the hermit and threatened to tell everybody, putting the worst possible construction on it. I would be disgraced and Brother Caspar banished. So I kept quiet. But it doesn't matter now – it's all over and I've no reason to be silent. If Rowland had treated me differently perhaps I would have taken another course of action.'

Lady Denby fought between her inclination to indulge in another tirade and her desire to hear the rest of Elinor's story. I saw her struggling for control and finally she blurted out: 'Go on!'

'I went into Ashdale early this morning and made some enquiries. At last I found out where Carrie was in lodgings; Rowland had moved her there when he realized the inn was too dangerous. I went to see her. She was very reluctant to confide in me at first but I told her she'd already been seen once in the park so it was time she introduced herself to her new family.'

'I did come once,' said Carrie, 'but when I saw the house I didn't know what to do – the stableboy said Rowland was out somewhere. He kept refusing to bring me here – he said he was waiting for the right time but I began to think the time was never going to be right.'

'A clandestine marriage!' cried Louisa Thorpe. 'You must find that romantic, Amelia. Your novels are full of clandestine marriages.'

'Perhaps, but they don't involve publicans' daughters.'

'And where does Mr Tyler come into this farrago?' enquired Mrs Thorpe, with a coy look in his direction.

'I went to the Unicorn for something to eat.' George spoke without looking at her, directing his answer towards Amelia Denby. 'On the way out I met Rowland and asked if his sister had been found. He said she'd never been lost and he'd come to hire a gig to take her back to Lovegrove. I said I'd accompany them and I went back to his wife's lodgings and heard the whole story.'

'And I am not just a girl or a woman or a mere publican's daughter!' declared Carrie defiantly. 'I am Mrs Webb, if you please.'

'A disgrace to the name!' exclaimed Lady Denby, who, after all, had once been Mrs Webb herself. 'Rowland's father was a gentleman and a man of property. Heaven knows what Sir Ralph will say. A shock like this is enough to carry him off!'

I reflected that Rowland was merely a stepson and Sir Ralph, whose first wife was a brewer's daughter, was unlikely to be as horrified as her ladyship.

'Rowland,' she ordered, 'will you kindly remove your wife and child from my presence – they are a continual reminder of the shame you have brought on us all.'

'You might at least let us stay the night,' he protested.

'I wouldn't stay if you paid me,' declared Carrie. 'Come on, Rowley, let's get back to our lodgings and then we can make plans.'

'No doubt, Rowland,' said Lady Denby with heavy sarcasm, 'your father-in-law can give you employment as a pot-boy. You'll need some means of earning a living when your allowance is cancelled.'

'What – but I'm entitled—'

'To nothing. Your father left very little but debts and I've had to support both of us by the labour of my pen and a small annuity. I owe you nothing now. Please go!'

Rowland looked as though he might prolong his pleading and begged his mother to see him alone but she remained adamant and Carrie swept out of the hall ahead of him leaving him little option but to follow her.

Lady Denby suddenly descended on Sophie, who backed nervously away.

'He has broken my heart!' she cried. 'And yours too, I know, you poor child – all your affections wasted and your hopes dashed by that deceiver!'

Sophie looked at her with astonishment and some alarm, when she found herself pressed to Lady Denby's heaving bosom.

'Unhappy girl! I know what it is to suffer. You must be brave. And now I must go and lie down. I am sorry to abandon my guests but I cannot face dinner. This has been an appalling day.'

She wished us all good evening and departed. I later saw a heavily laden tray being taken to her room. We had all watched, breathless, as if at a play. When the leading lady departed there was an outburst of animated conversation.

'She seems to think I was besotted with Rowland!' cried Sophie.

'That's what she planned, so she believes it happened,' I said. I went over to Elinor. 'Everyone is very glad to see you safely home,' I told her. 'We were all very concerned.'

'Yes, and I'm so sorry about poor Papa.'

'You could simply have *told* your stepmother about Rowland's marriage.'

'Oh yes, that's that I was going to do at first but then Rowland and his mother were so horrid to me I decided to cause the greatest amount of trouble possible. I thought an actual confrontation would be much more exciting than a mere denunciation. I quite enjoyed it.'

'I'm sure you did. I think we all did if truth be told.'

'Of course, I knew I was going to make an escape with you and your brother. Now I can't come – not while Papa is so ill.'

'We can wait a few days, I'm sure. Your father will soon be on the mend and he'll want you to have a holiday.'

I little realized then that our departure would be delayed by something far more dramatic than Elinor's reluctance to leave her sick father.

There were only six of us at dinner and without our host and hostess the meal lost its formality. We all moved to one end of the table, George carefully manoeuvring himself away from the seat next to Mrs Thorpe; and the conversation became general.

'Did any of you, apart from Elinor, have any idea Rowland was married?' enquired Louisa.

'Aunt Charlotte and I thought something suspicious was

going on,' said Sophie. 'We saw him going into a cottage in Ashdale near that nice bonnet shop. We thought he had a mistress in there.'

'Sophie!' I remonstrated.

'Well, we did.'

'I don't think Amelia would have been nearly so distressed if the female in question had been a mistress,' said Mrs Thorpe. 'Mistresses can usually be bought off but a wife and child are really too much to stomach.'

'Do you think she'll come round eventually?' asked Frank.

'Oh yes. Amelia adores Rowland – he's her only child after all and she's always spoiled and indulged him. I'm sure if he lies low for a while he can start edging his way back into her affections. They've had rows before, though none as bad as this, and they've always made it up. He usually knows how to win her round.'

'I wish Lady Denby didn't suppose I nurtured some sort of romantic interest in Rowland,' said Sophie. 'He and I were never more than friends, and he's not at all the sort of man I want to marry.'

'Of course not, dear, we all understand,' said Louisa Thorpe. 'I think Amelia entertained hopes in that direction but I could tell you weren't suited. He had to pretend an interest in you to hide the true situation. Perhaps he regrets now his haste in a choice of bride – one forced on him after giving way to a reckless impulse.'

'I think Colonel Hartley suspected something,' said Sophie thoughtfully. 'He once said that one day Rowland might surprise us all.'

'The Colonel is very perceptive,' observed Elinor, 'I think he knows more than we suppose about a great many matters.' After this enigmatic remark she fell silent.

'Well, our numbers are sadly depleted this evening and likely to shrink even more,' said Frank Lawrence. 'I will be departing shortly.'

'Really?' Louisa Thorpe looked shocked. 'You've not said anything to me.'

He shrugged. 'We don't have to make our plans together, surely, Aunt? You may stay as long as you please. Lady Denby is your friend after all. I have my own life to lead and I must return to town very soon. It will only be for a few days but I have some business to transact that has already been delayed too long.'

'If it is only for a few days . . .'

'Of course.'

'We're going as soon as Sir Ralph is better and Elinor feels able to leave him,' said George. 'I must say, I'm beginning to long for home. Too much excitement doesn't suit me.'

There was something wrong; I felt it. Mrs Thorpe was still looking at Frank with a sort of stifled fury. I thought what he had said was in no way remarkable. Why should an active young man be content to stay kicking his heels in the house of strangers who were nothing to him, dancing attendance on an aunt and no doubt growing more bored every day? Yet Louisa Thorpe still looked incredulous. She obviously felt that Frank ought to have confided in her before making an announcement to everyone else but he seemed to think it of no importance.

I wondered again about George's change of mind regarding Mrs Thorpe. There was something going on of which I knew nothing.

After dinner, instead of dividing, we all repaired to

the library. 'This is a pleasant change,' observed Frank Lawrence, sitting beside me. Out of the corner of my eye I saw George take Sophie by the arm and beckon Elinor to join them as he inspected a large book of engravings on the library table. I am sure he was not much interested but it served to deflect the possible attentions of Louisa Thorpe, who decided to await the arrival of tea in solitary grandeur.

'I believe she is offended with me,' murmured Frank, 'she thinks I should stay to keep her company.'

'She can hardly expect to control your comings and goings,' I said, 'and the Denbys are her friends, not yours. She came here on her own last time.'

'That is so, but Sir Ralph's illness and Lady Denby's pre-occupations will make it lonely for her. She can't bear to feel neglected.'

'But you have your own life to lead. I think it's perfectly understandable that you should want to get away. You must find Lovegrove quite tedious, despite recent events.'

'I'm glad you understand that.'

'I believe you and Sophie enjoyed yourselves this after-noon,' I said, changing the subject.

'Yes indeed; she really is a most delightful girl. Some of the credit must go to you.'

'I hardly think so. Both her parents were sweet-natured, charming people.'

'But you have nurtured her talents. You have taught her music and drawing and made her read and enjoy reading. She's no fool.'

'And you have just discovered that?'

He smiled ruefully. 'I thought Rowland was a lucky fellow. Now I realize what an idiot he is.'

'I hope you are not going to force me into the difficult position of having to warn you off?'

'Of course not. I know she's not for me, and pretty and captivating as she is, I've always preferred more mature women.'

'Am I to take that as a compliment?'

'Oh, I think so, don't you? I shall miss you.' His hand pressed mine.

'Thank you,' I said gently disengaging his grasp, 'but I may well be gone before you return.'

'Then we must hope to meet again one day. Who can tell what lies ahead? "What's to come is still unsure".'

'"Youth's a stuff will not endure",' I added.

'You've left out the kiss. "Then come kiss me, sweet and twenty".'

'But I'm nearer thirty, Mr Lawrence. Go and amuse Sophie.'

The two of them settled to a game of backgammon as George hastily joined me. There was a great deal of laughter and joking accusations as they both cheated shamelessly. Mrs Thorpe glared at them with undisguised resentment.

'At least they're enjoying themselves,' said George gloomily, 'which is more than can be said for anyone else.'

Tea was handed round and then Elinor excused herself as she was understandably very tired and wished to rest. George was reluctant to play cards as it would involve Mrs Thorpe and with Elinor's departure there was no longer a four for whist.

The backgammon came to an end and there were many smothered yawns and sighs as we turned over books. In the end we all retired early after a somewhat skimpy supper.

# CHAPTER FIFTEEN

The next day Sir Ralph was much better and was sitting up in bed complaining of the gruel with which he was being fed. Elinor brought up the local newspaper and started reading it to him but they were interrupted by Lady Denby, who was in a thoroughly bad mood. She declared she had not slept a wink all night, had a splitting headache and was surrounded by people who seemed determined to provoke her.

Her tirade was not guaranteed to provide peace and quiet for the invalid and she finally broke down and sobbed that she and her son were parted forever by his unpardonable conduct. Sir Ralph bore all this remarkably well. He did not seem unduly distressed by news of his stepson's transgression.

'Stop fretting, Amelia, there's nothing we can do about it. The girl may not be so bad after all.'

'You haven't seen her. A vulgar little minx! Obviously she couldn't wait to get him into her clutches – she and her grasping family.'

'I don't know about grasping – not if they knew Rowland has very little money. Perhaps they were misled—'

At this point Elinor slipped out of the room so we never

knew what was said next but soon afterwards the doctor arrived, pronounced Sir Ralph 'on the mend', and bled him again, which made him sleep fitfully for most of the day.

Lady Denby next chose to quarrel publicly with her friend Louisa whom she accused of gloating over her misfortune. 'You've never had children yourself so you cannot possibly understand.'

'I *do* understand. It's been a blow to your pride. You hoped to secure an heiress – that's the only reason you invited the Tylers. You hoped he'd take up with little Sophie. I'd say she's had a lucky escape.'

'How dare you! Really, Louisa, you go too far.'

'Not quite far enough perhaps. Everyone else is afraid to tell you the truth – that's why Rowland kept his marriage a secret for so long.'

'No, it is you who are unwilling to face the truth. Your nephew left for London this morning before breakfast. Did he even trouble to wish you goodbye?'

The colour drained from Mrs Thorpe's face and for a few moments she could not speak. 'He said he was going,' she murmured, 'it's only for a few days. He has business to attend to. I suppose I must go too; I can see I've outstayed my welcome. I must return to my humble cottage and a solitary life.'

'Your life has never been solitary, Louisa. Oh come now,' Lady Denby saw that her friend's lip was trembling, 'cheer up – if you had only half my troubles you'd feel a great deal better.'

'At least you can be miserable in comfort,' gulped Mrs Thorpe, pulling out a lacy handkerchief and applying it carefully to each eye.

'Why, so can you, if you stay here with us.'

So the quarrel passed over but left an uneasy atmosphere. Later that day my brother told me that Louisa Thorpe had made an attempt to renew her flirtation with him. He sheepishly told me that she had trapped him in an alcove in the corridor as he was going to his room.

'I told her to forget me,' he said, 'that I knew all about her and did not wish to continue our acquaintance, let alone allow it to progress further.'

'And what was her reaction?'

'Oh, she was angry. Hell hath no fury and all that.'

Sophie and I went out for our walk a little later than usual but when we saw Rowland approaching on horseback she hastily excused herself and ran back to the house. I awaited his approach and greeted him with what I thought to be the right amount of civility.

'Good morning, Mr Webb – I wasn't expecting to see you here today.'

He dismounted. 'Miss Tyler, perhaps you can help me.'

'I'm not at all sure I should.'

'I only mean with advice. Carrie wants us to go straight back to London – in fact we got as far as the Unicorn and then saw the Mail leave with Frank Lawrence perched on top.'

'Yes, he's going away for a few days.'

'I thought all along we ought not to do anything in a hurry. I managed to convince her it was worth waiting another week at least. I know what my mother is like – she was in a fury yesterday but there's a chance she'll come round once she's calmed down. I've told Carrie it's better for her to keep out of the way until I've won over Mama. Perhaps you can tell me how she is this morning. Do you think it would be worth trying to see her?'

I shook my head. 'Not today – she's still in a very bad mood and was quite unpleasant to Mrs Thorpe in front of everybody. She did, however, attempt some sort of reconciliation without going so far as to apologize.'

'I feared it might be so. How is Sir Ralph?'

'Considerably better, I believe. The doctor came and bled him again, which has laid him low for the time being. Your Mama told him about your marriage and it didn't carry him off as she feared – in fact he didn't seem greatly perturbed at all from what I've heard. I can't really see why he should be as you're not his son.'

'Wish I was – he's a good-natured old boy. But I'll keep away from my mother today. Incidentally I – I hope Sophie wasn't too upset – I saw her running off. . . .'

'Oh, I think that was mere embarrassment – she wasn't at all disappointed, you know. She thought of you only as a friend.'

'Ah yes.' He looked troubled. I wondered if he had secretly hoped Sophie was smitten or if he was wishing he was still unattached and free to pursue pretty girls of good family.

'I've left a lot of my things here,' he said. 'I wasn't expecting to be thrown out in such a hurry. I thought if I went in through the servants' quarters I could get one of them to collect what I need and send it on to our lodgings.'

I nodded and about to move away when he said: 'There's a strange man at the Unicorn – came up from Devon. He looks like a lawyer or something of that sort – dressed in black and very respectable. He's been asking about Lovegrove and Colonel Hartley and other matters of that sort. I didn't speak to him because I didn't want to get involved – I've enough to engage me at present and he'll find out all he wants easily enough.'

He hesitated. 'Er – you won't mention to my mother that I've been here?'

'Of course not.'

'Well, I must be off.' He touched his hat, remounted and rode across the grass to the side of the house.

The rest of the day passed without incident.

The Hartleys had heard of events at Lovegrove and sent a sympathetic note with a basket of fruit from their hothouse.

Lady Denby spent most of the time in her study, toiling over her novel.

Louisa Thorpe moped about the house, apparently unable to settle to any occupation. It was on one of these wanderings that the encounter with my brother took place. He immediately went out for a ride and came back late in the afternoon, tired, wet and dismal.

Elinor, after spending the morning playing the piano, joined Sophie and me after luncheon. As the day had turned dull and showery we occupied ourselves in embroidery and sketching.

Dusk was falling and candles were being lit after dinner when we were disturbed by a commotion in the entrance hall – an hysterical sobbing and wailing. As on the previous evening we had repaired to the library so we were aware of the noise outside the door.

'Whatever is that caterwauling?' demanded Lady Denby, going to the door herself to investigate. The butler was endeavouring to calm an obviously terrified housemaid who, oblivious to both soothing words and commands, sank onto one of the hall chairs and buried in her head in her hands.

'What is going on?' enquired her ladyship.

The butler seemed exasperated. 'This foolish woman was sent into the village on an errand and coming through the park in the twilight she fancied she saw an – er – apparition.'

'I *did* see 'im – I *did*!' howled the girl.

'She had no business entering the house through the front door but—'

'It was 'alf open. I was scared to go round to the side door – I wanted to get safe indoors.'

'Stop snivelling and tell me what you saw,' ordered Lady Denby.

'The 'ermit – just as 'e was in that robe thing – gliding about among the trees.'

'Gliding?'

'I swear 'is feet didn't touch the grass. 'E floated towards the priory ruins then vanished into thin air. They say suicides come back to 'aunt us.'

I had seen the maid about the house – a rather pretty girl with fair curls escaping from her cap and plump, pink cheeks which were now excessively flushed, her china-blue eyes wide open. I thought she was overdoing the hysterics, obviously enjoying the attention she was attracting.

'Nonsense, Susan!' bellowed Lady Denby. 'Go back to your work immediately and try to calm yourself. And don't spread any stupid stories among the servants.'

This last order was impossible to enforce. Before the day was out everyone in the house had heard of the phantom hermit floating about the grounds. I was sure that before long there would be further reports of ghostly hermits. At the time I put it all down to fear, superstition and overactive imagination. I was wrong, of course.

# CHAPTER SIXTEEN

The next morning, George took Sophie for a drive in the gig so I was left to my own devices. I spent a while with Elinor and then went into the library on my own. I was sitting quietly reading when the door to Lady Denby's study suddenly swung open and a bundle of books and papers cascaded to the floor followed by a muffled oath from Colonel Hartley. It was obvious he had tried to open the door whilst still retaining his package. I at once leapt up to help him, wondering why Lady Denby had not followed him to the door to give assistance. I could see her sitting calmly at her desk. She glanced up briefly and then returned to her writing.

The Colonel thanked me and expressed his pleasure at seeing me still here. I explained about the delay caused by Sir Ralph's illness and he seemed curiously satisfied.

As I tidied up the pile of documents, I noticed with interest that there were two sketchbooks and many loose papers with drawings and writing.

'I think there is some string in the desk. Would it help if I tied these together for you?' I suggested.

'Why yes, I'm afraid I'm very clumsy at times.'

'No clumsier than most people with two arms. I couldn't

help seeing a little of your drawings – I presume they are yours. I would really like to look at them properly if I may.'

'Of course. Lady Denby doesn't find them of much use.'

He explained that her ladyship had asked him to give her advice on her portrayal of Spain in her new novel. 'I'm afraid my contribution to her research was not to her liking. She seems to think that the whole of Spain is covered with lofty, precipitous mountains inhabited by tall dark bandits with flashing eyes. She could scarcely believe me when I told her some of it was flat and the bandits I'd seen – those who'd joined the guerrillas, anyway – were mostly short, coarse and smelling of garlic. They did appalling things to their poor captives which I couldn't possibly describe but I could tell none of it was romantic enough for her taste.'

'All her heroes have flashing eyes,' I said, 'and they are all intolerably noble. It's no use trying to bring a little reality into her inventions. She'll go her own way in the end and I'm sure her readers would be very disappointed if her bandit hero was short and coarse and smelt of garlic.'

'Yes, I suppose so. She retained a third sketchbook which belonged to a friend of mine who was killed in the Pyrenees. He was very good at drawing people: peasants, guerrillas, pretty dancers, ragged urchins, muleteers – anyone at all picturesque, so she may be able to make use of that.'

'Meanwhile, before I tie up the parcel for you, could I see your sketches?'

'Of course, but they are mainly dull pictures of fortifications and terrain.'

We sat on the sofa and went through his sketchbooks together. He did not launch into descriptions of campaigns but added a detail here and there:

'Talavera – the battlefield; very flat and dull! Salamanca ditto; nothing exciting could happen in such a place.'

His work was careful and meticulous but, as he admitted, competent rather than talented.

'Badajos,' he said quietly, shuffling through some of the loose papers. 'That's the walls before the siege – this other one is very rough and shows one of the breaches after we captured the city.'

'Is that where Harry O'Neill died?'

He nodded. 'And he's buried nearby with other officers. I'm sorry – does that distress you?'

I shook my head. '"Old unhappy far-off things and battles long ago?" It doesn't cause pain any more, only sadness.'

We sat companionably talking for the next half-hour until we were interrupted by Lady Denby, who came charging in from her study.

'What, are you still here, Colonel Hartley? I thought you were going on to Ashdale.'

'So I am, but there is no hurry. My conversation with Miss Tyler here is more amusing and interesting than anything Ashdale has to offer.'

'I see.' She regarded me narrowly. 'It's nearly time for luncheon, will you stay?'

He declined the invitation and said he would go up to see Sir Ralph for ten minutes and then ride on to Ashdale where he could transact his business in the afternoon after getting a bite to eat at the Unicorn. He smiled at me and took his leave.

'Well,' said Amelia Denby, 'you seem to know how to engage the interest of the military.'

'Yes,' I said, 'I have some knowledge of the life.'

'Really?' She looked interested but I told her no more.

A few minutes later, after her ladyship had gone back to her study, it occurred to me that I had not told Colonel Hartley about the 'apparition' supposedly seen in the park. I went out into the entrance hall just as he was coming downstairs. He hailed me cheerfully and informed me that Sir Ralph seemed much better and was complaining about his food.

'That's always a good sign,' he said. 'I told him not to start eating beefsteaks but to stick to lighter meals for a little longer. I don't see why he can't have fish or eggs but I suppose the doctor will have the last word. He told me about Rowland but I already knew – in fact I've suspected some time that there was a woman in the case – I've seen him lurking around Ashdale looking furtive on more than one occasion.'

'You are very observant. There was something I forgot to tell you – I don't suppose it's of any great importance but I think you ought to know.'

When I told him about the phantom hermit his reaction surprised me as he seemed to take it seriously.

'Surely you don't think it was a ghost?'

'No, of course not but if it *wasn't* a figment of the girl's imagination then it may well be of significance.'

At that moment Mrs Thorpe came into the hall. 'Ah, there you are, Colonel Hartley!' she cried. 'And Miss Tyler – I hope I haven't interrupted a tête-à-tête.'

'Not at all,' I said, 'I was just telling the Colonel about the maid thinking she saw Brother Caspar's ghost.'

'Silly creature! They are all superstitious. Colonel, may I have a word? Excuse me dear,' she smirked.

I particularly disliked being addressed as 'dear' by a patronizing woman whose alliance with an ugly old man apparently entitled her to look down on me. She drew the Colonel to one side and spent some time murmuring in his ear. I saw his face change, then she attempted to squeeze his arm, encountered an empty sleeve and hastily snatched her hand away; then she recovered and patted him on the shoulder in a familiar fashion.

'What did she want?' I enquired when she had gone.

'You don't like her, I know.'

'Who does? My brother George has changed from admiration to loathing but won't tell me why. I'm greatly relieved and I've no doubt I'll get it out of him eventually – he won't be able to keep it to himself indefinitely.'

'She told me that she possibly had something of great importance to tell me but privacy was essential and she hoped to see me later when we can be alone.'

'Take care,' I said. 'Having lost George she may set her cap at you.'

'I'll be on my guard. I've dealt with surprise attacks before. But I really must go now. I'm glad you'll be here a little longer.'

I hastily picked up the parcel of books and papers which he had left on the hall table and preceded him through the front door. Then I insisted on putting them in his saddle-bag for him.

He smiled and thanked me. 'You think of everything. I'm beginning to wonder what I'd do without you. Goodbye, my dear.'

He rode off up the drive towards the gate. His final words with the last affectionate expression had taken me by surprise. They were little more than courtesy – quite slight and trivial yet they set my heart pounding.

# CHAPTER SEVENTEEN

The night was thundery again. I lay in bed a long time, unable to sleep, seeing the room illuminated by sudden flashes of lightning and counting the seconds to the next rumble of thunder, which came nearer and nearer. There were other noises too; creaking floorboards, footsteps, low voices and the opening and closing of doors, as though the whole house was restless and all its occupants on the move.

The storm broke with great ferocity but gradually ran its course and finally rolled away, leaving behind heavy, drumming rain. I slept at last, shallowly and fitfully, only to be woken by another sound. At first I thought the storm had returned but the noise that woke me was not like thunder – more like a soft, heavy thudding within the house. I heard doors opening, voices calling and then a shrill scream.

Hastily I jumped out of bed, snatched up my dressing gown and ran to the door. I found Sophie standing in the passage outside.

'What was it, Aunt Charlotte? There was the strangest sound, like something heavy tumbling – as though someone had thrown a sack of potatoes downstairs.' She was closer to the truth than either of us imagined.

The main staircase at Lovegrove was of oak, well polished and uncarpeted. The hall below was paved with ancient flagstones. Most of the house's occupants had been raised from their sleep and we gathered on landing and stairs in a variety of dressing gowns and shawls. Those who had lighted candles lent the flames to those who had not and a sinister, flickering glow illuminated the scene.

At the foot of the stairs, lying on the flagstones in a curiously twisted position was a body in a white nightgown. For a few seconds I could scarcely think who it might be. Then I saw the mane of dark hair, the small bare feet, the plump arms with dimpled elbows. It was Louisa Thorpe. Lady Denby was leaning over her, trying to rouse her.

'Louisa – wake up, dear. Speak to me. Bring water, someone, and sal volatile. She's quite unconscious. Brandy too – and hurry!'

My brother George had gone down to join her and more candles were brought from adjoining rooms. Despite his occasional foolishness he was not lacking in acumen and he had the merit of keeping his head in a crisis.

'She's not unconscious, she's dead,' he said gravely. 'There's a nasty wound on her head and blood on the floor. She must have hit the stone with some force.' He bent and felt her pulse. 'It could be she broke her neck in the fall,' he added. 'You'd better send for your doctor to certify the cause of death.'

'She can't be dead!' cried Lady Denby. 'She *can't* be! I'm sure she'll revive if we apply a few appropriate remedies. And Louisa, don't lie there like that. What were you doing, wandering about in the middle of the night?'

'I expect she was disturbed by the storm,' said George.

'Perhaps she thought she heard a strange noise and came to the top of the stairs to see and missed her footing on the half-landing.'

I thought it was odd she hadn't put on a dressing gown or at least thrown a shawl round her shoulders but it was a warm night and perhaps she had amorous intentions. I could imagine her slipping through George's door: 'Oh, Mr Tyler, I am so frightened – I have always been terrified of thunderstorms.' But there were two things wrong with this theory: there would be no need for her to go downstairs and the storm was over when she fell.

Lady Denby insisted on Louisa being carried to her room and placed on her bed. The room was near the top of the stairs and next but one to mine. The door stood open and I went in and found the chamber candlestick unlit by her bed so I used my own candle to light it. A tinderbox lay beside it – why hadn't she used it? Perhaps there had been no time, but it was hardly surprising she had slipped in the darkness.

Another thing I noticed: Louisa Thorpe had been sleeping in a double bed with two pillows and a bolster. One of the pillows was covered by a linen case with a heavy lace border; the other pillowcase was missing.

It seemed obvious to me from the lolling head of the dead woman that she had indeed broken her neck, though there was also a patch of bloody, matted hair on her head that showed the site of a violent blow. Oddly enough I was not nearly so upset by Louisa Thorpe's demise as I had been by the death of the hermit. Perhaps it was because I was surrounded by other people and my brother's calmness was reassuring: also – I had to admit it – because I disliked the woman so much.

Lady Denby despatched a manservant to fetch Dr Stringer and proceeded to try all the usual methods of reviving an unconscious person. I fetched Mrs Thorpe's mirror from her dressing table and held it to her nose and mouth.

'Look,' I said, 'it's quite clear.'

'Let me see,' said Lady Denby, holding it so close that it was immediately clouded by her own breath.

'Nonsense – she's still alive!'

There followed a series of ridiculous attempts to restore Louisa Thorpe to life. Much as I had disliked the woman I did not like to see her subjected to these futile efforts; far better to cover her with a sheet and await the doctor. But Lady Denby had to have her way. She snatched a feather from one of Louisa's bonnets and set fire to it, hoping the fumes wafted past her friend's nose might rouse her. She chafed her hands, bathed her brow with cold water, tried to force brandy between her lips, called for mustard poultices which were not forthcoming and finally, exhausted by her efforts and with hopes at last extinguished, she collapsed sobbing at the foot of the bed.

'Did anyone suffer so many tragedies in so short a space?' she wailed. 'First the hermit, then Sir Ralph, then Rowland, now Louisa – all gone!'

'I'm not gone,' said a voice from the doorway.

'Oh, Ralphy, I'm so desolate!' she cried, rushing to enfold him in a smothering embrace.

'Poor Melly, you've had a terrible time,' he said, patting her soothingly.

She recovered a little and at once took charge of his welfare. 'You ought not to be out of bed, Ralphy – go back to it at once.'

'I'm all right, just a little weak and shaky and that's due to being bled and not having enough to eat. I take it Louisa fell downstairs. What was she doing in the middle of the night?'

'Just what we were all wondering,' said George. 'Where was she going? What had she heard?'

Sir Ralph was persuaded to return to bed but the rest of us found it impossible despite the fact that it was after three in the morning. I suggested to Sophie that she really ought to go and lie down but she declared she could not rest.

'I'm wide awake now. I can't possibly sleep again, there's too much going on.'

Elinor disappeared, however. She had not said a word.

Dr Stringer arrived at last looking decidedly weary and ill-tempered. He confirmed what we already knew – that Mrs Thorpe had broken her neck and had a severe contusion on the side of her head.

'Probably some more broken bones, I shouldn't wonder, but I can't say more until I have a proper look in daylight. You'd better get Colonel Hartley over here tomorrow and he'll inform the coroner.'

'Not another post-mortem and inquest?' cried Lady Denby. 'Oh, the shame and horror! It's more than I can bear! And what about her family? If only Frank hadn't gone away! Louisa's parents are dead but I suppose I could contact her eldest sister. The one who married a clergyman. That's Mrs Lawrence, Frank's mother. She must be told. I think Louisa had her address written somewhere – she was writing her a letter the other day. What a dreadful shock for the poor woman – not that I know much about her. They were all girls in that family and she was the eldest and Louisa the youngest so they were never really close. But at times like these, blood is thicker than water.'

'You don't know where the nephew is?' asked the doctor.

'No, he went up to London. He'll be very upset – he was very attached to his aunt – more so than to his mother.'

As it was now nearly four in the morning, Dr Stringer was asked to spend the rest of the night in the house as it was hardly worth his making the journey home. We all repaired to our rooms to await the morning. A servant was despatched before breakfast to inform Colonel Hartley of the night's tragedy and to ask him to come over as soon as possible.

# CHAPTER EIGHTEEN

We were eating breakfast when Colonel Hartley arrived. At least, the Tyler family ate breakfast; our hosts both had trays taken up to their rooms. I at once ran out into the hall to meet our visitor, followed by my brother.

'I'm thinking of renting a room here,' smiled the Colonel, 'and you must forgive me for appearing flippant but I have never before encountered such a series of events. If it weren't so tragic it would be almost comical. But first, I'd like to talk to you and hear what you experienced last night. Then I'll have a word with Dr Stringer and view the remains. Where did the accident take place?' Then he added, speaking to me in an undertone, 'Assuming it *was* an accident.'

We showed him exactly where Mrs Thorpe was found. I provided him with a sketch I had made before breakfast showing the position of the body. Lady Denby suddenly appeared at the top of the stairs striking a dramatic attitude with the back of her right hand pressed to her forehead and the left clutching her heart.

'Dear Colonel Hartley, I have supped full of horrors! That you should be called on yet again to investigate the dreadful events at this unhappy house! It is beyond all endurance!'

152

'If you'd please come down, ma'am, perhaps you can tell me what you witnessed as I understand you were one of the first people on the scene.'

'Indeed, it was I who raised the alarm. I was unable to sleep owing to the violence of the storm so I lit my candles on the little desk in my room and devoted an hour to writing. I was disturbed by the sound of someone falling and I took up a candle and went to see what was happening. I could see my poor friend lying at the foot of these stairs: immobile – shattered – life extinguished!' Her voice choked and she came gliding downstairs, taking care to hold onto the banisters with one hand.

Dr Stringer emerged from the library, where he had been sleeping on the sofa, looking bleary-eyed and unshaven.

'Oh, poor Dr Stringer!' cried Lady Denby. 'You look in need of hot water and a razor. I'll see they are provided. You can use my room now I have risen. Then there's plenty to eat and drink set out in the breakfast room.'

The doctor exchanged a few words with Colonel Hartley, who assured him that there was no great need for haste, and he was conducted upstairs by her ladyship, who promised to provide him with one of Sir Ralph's razors.

'I'd rather take a look first on my own,' said Colonel Hartley. 'I don't find the good doctor altogether helpful. If you'd come with me I'd be grateful for your help.'

He addressed George and me but my brother, to my relief, excused himself, anxious to return to his breakfast and not too keen to see Louisa again, dead or alive.

'I'm sure Charlotte will be more use to you than I could be,' he said. 'She was helping Lady Denby from the first.'

The Colonel and I went up to Louisa Thorpe's room

together. The corpse was now decently draped in a sheet. I pointed out the oddities I had observed: the fact she had not lit a candle, the missing pillowcase and the fact she had not put on her dressing gown or shawl.

'I did wonder if she was going to make a last attempt on my brother,' I said, 'perhaps pretending to be frightened by the storm, but it was over before she had the fall and she was nowhere near his room. No one has any idea what she was doing prowling about the house in the middle of the night.'

'I don't think it matters much. I think the missing pillow-case could prove more important.'

'Why?'

'Well, do you really believe Mrs Thorpe's death was an accident?'

'What else could it be?'

'You noticed a number of curious features. Do they suggest anything untoward?'

He looked around the room and took a heavy brass candlestick over to the window, asking me to bring the other. After looking at both carefully he turned his attention to the marble obelisks above the fireplace. I carried them both over to him and he gave an exclamation of triumph.

'Here we are! There is the faintest trace of dried blood on this one – can you see it?'

'I think so. *Is* it blood?'

'I'm pretty sure of it, though it's the merest trace. When wiping something clean by candlelight it is difficult to be exact.'

'You think it was used to strike Mrs Thorpe?'

'Possibly. Then the pillowcase was used to wipe it clean

and then wrapped round the poor woman's head until she was carried to the top of the stairs and then thrown down. She was a small woman and a strong man – even a tall, strong woman – could have done it.'

I shuddered.

'I'm sorry – am I distressing you? I've seen too much of death, perhaps.'

'No. I disliked the woman but I would never have wished her such a death.'

'It is, perhaps, a consequence of what has gone before. This may not be a succession of separate events but a connected series perpetrated by one diseased mind.'

'Then there's a connection between everything that's happened?'

'I'm inclined to think so.'

'A madman?'

'I wouldn't go so far as to say that. There's logic and intelligence at work. There are certain people – quite pleasant and plausible on the surface – who have no sense of right and wrong. They are interested only in their own advantage and destroy everyone who stands in their way.'

'It can't be anyone in this house, surely?'

'I don't know anything for certain.'

There was a small writing table in the room set out with pen, ink and stationery. A few letters lay on top of it, which he glanced at curiously, then he opened one of the drawers, glanced down into it with a frown, then picked up some sort of folded document which he thrust inside his coat.

I was about to question him when Lady Denby charged in, followed by Dr Stringer.

'What are you doing here, Miss Tyler?' she demanded.

'What possible use could you be to Colonel Hartley? I should have thought you'd be more of a hindrance than a help.'

'She has been of the greatest possible assistance,' said Colonel Hartley.

'Well, I'm afraid her usefulness is at an end as Dr Stringer is here to look at poor Louisa. It was impossible to carry out a proper examination by candlelight. Come, Miss Tyler, this is no place for us poor women.' She ushered me out of the room and we left the two men to their work.

'Do you like Colonel Hartley?' she asked me as we went downstairs.

'Of course,' I replied in as calm a tone as possible. 'What is there *not* to like?'

'That's not quite what I meant.'

'No? Then I am baffled.'

'Oh, come now, you are not usually so obtuse. I meant, do you like him in a way exceeding ordinary friendship?'

'I'm not at all sure what you mean, even now. He is a most agreeable man and I'm sure you think so too.'

She sighed. 'Very well, keep your own counsel if you wish. I am never one to interfere, but mind what you are about, that's all.'

With that she returned to the breakfast room to impose her presence on my brother and Sophie. The latter soon joined me for our morning walk and was eager to know what had transpired.

'Lady Denby must be really upset,' she said, 'she ate nothing but a little toast and half a boiled egg.'

'That's because she had a breakfast tray carried up to her an hour ago.'

'The old fraud! I don't believe half she says, do you? But do tell me what Colonel Hartley thinks about it all.'

I could not tell her much about his theories. He had entrusted me with opinions that were not, at this stage, intended for anyone else, so I told her as much as I could and said a walk in the fresh air was the best thing for us both after the horrors of the night. We were returning to the house just as Colonel Hartley was leaving.

'We've done all we can do for now,' he said. 'The doctor is attending to Sir Ralph. I'm riding to Ashdale. I might as well inform the coroner myself and make arrangements for a post-mortem and inquest if necessary. I'm sure the verdict will be accidental death or misadventure.'

'I'm tired,' said Sophie. 'I'll go in and have a rest, Aunt Charlotte, if you don't mind.' She gave me a sly look; obviously she was deliberately intending to leave me in the Colonel's company. As he was heading for the gates we walked there together, he leading his horse.

'Are you sure you're not tired too?' he enquired. 'You had little sleep last night.'

'No, not at all. You must have had many sleepless nights when you were campaigning.'

'I suppose so, but ladies are not used to that sort of thing – well, maybe a few of them are but violent events in a quiet country house are more of a shock because they are so incongruous.'

'What does Dr Stringer think?'

'Oh, it was certainly an accident: she had no light and the stairs were slippery. The good doctor looks no further than that. It was the same with my poor friend Rushworth. . . . To tell the truth,' he continued after a pause, 'I don't like to think of you and Sophie in that house.'

'What could possibly happen to us? My brother George is a perfectly adequate guardian. Surely you don't think Sophie and I are likely to fall downstairs in the middle of the night?'

'No, the same thing won't happen twice but there may be other dangers. I'm sorry, I can't be more specific. If I knew what they were I might warn you of them. It's better that you don't know too much at present.'

'Now you are talking in riddles.'

He looked at me with a serious expression. His eyes were perfectly grey, I thought, with not a trace of blue or green.

'I will tell you this much,' he said, 'because I trust you to keep it to yourself. When I was searching Mrs Thorpe's desk this morning I found a letter addressed to me and inscribed: "To be opened in the event of my death!" I have it here, as yet unread, but it may provide us with some answers. It may be the coroner should see it.

'I shall see you later today and let you all know what is to happen concerning the post-mortem and inquest. Goodbye for now.'

He hesitated a moment and then kissed my hand and rode off at a brisk canter. His lips brushed against my ring and I recollected that Harry had kissed it before he put it on my finger. Somehow that gesture had brought the two of them together.

# CHAPTER NINETEEN

The news of Mrs Thorpe's death soon spread throughout the neighbourhood. As expected, gossip and rumour added all manner of embellishments. She had seen a ghostly apparition of the hermit and missed her footing as a result of shock; she had been sleepwalking; she had tripped whilst fleeing the intentions of an amorous guest. Who? I wondered; my poor brother seemed to be the only candidate.

Rowland got to hear of it and came riding over to find out what had really happened and also to make another attempt at a reconciliation with his mother.

Lady Denby was, I think, genuinely distressed by the death of her friend. She was by no means lacking in feeling despite her blustering, high-handed manner and she had already been shaken by Rowland's revelations and Sir Ralph's illness. Rowland hoped her misery might soften her heart and make her more amiably disposed towards him. He slipped in through a side door and went up to see Sir Ralph first and perhaps, I suspected, negotiate a loan if the old man was sufficiently recovered to sanction it. However, he found Elinor reading to her father and she swiftly showed him the door.

Next Rowland sought out his mother, who was in the process of writing a difficult letter to Louisa's sister, Mrs Lawrence. She rose in fury, berating him for bringing disgrace on the family and everlasting suffering to herself. She told him to go away and never return, and then, as he turned towards the door, she called him back, burst into tears, embraced him and begged him not to forsake her.

I heard all this when I encountered Rowland leaving his mother's study. He was so obviously relieved and pleased and longing to tell someone that he poured it all out to me.

'Of course, I've got to tread carefully and I scarcely dare mention Carrie. She won't have her in the house but at least she wants me back. It's a beginning. I'm to stay here tonight in my old room. She says she wants another man in the house now Sir Ralph is incapacitated. Carrie won't be too happy about that. I'm going back now to explain everything to her but we can't afford to be on bad terms with my mother, especially now there's little Arabella's future to consider.

'I say,' he added, turning on the way to the door. 'What a dreadful business about Louisa Thorpe. That must have been an awful shock for Mama. I think that's what softened her up so it's done me some good at least.'

How typical of Rowland, I thought, that his view of a sudden death was coloured by how it affected himself.

Later that day Colonel Hartley returned with the coroner, Dr Stringer and another doctor from Ashdale who had been called on to perform the autopsy on Mrs Thorpe. The coroner wished to see the scene of the death and inspect the corpse, which was then removed to the laundry.

When the coroner had departed, Colonel Hartley sought

me out and asked me to accompany him up to Mrs Thorpe's room.

'You were there last night,' he said, 'and also this morning in my company and you are sharp-eyed and observant. I want you to look round carefully and give me your opinion.'

We entered the room and I stood by the bed, looking at everything we had seen that morning.

'It seems to me,' I said, 'that several things have been moved very slightly – particularly the obelisks over the fireplace.'

'Yes, that's what I thought. And you remember I found faint traces of blood on one of them? Now there's nothing.'

'You mean someone's been in here and wiped it clean?'

'Exactly! Now see the writing-table. The letter she wrote to me was in the left-hand drawer. I closed it firmly after removing the document but now it is protruding about half an inch.'

'Was anything disturbed by the coroner or doctors?'

'No, I was present all the time.'

'Have you read the letter?'

'Oh yes, and I'll let you see it when the time is right. It confirms the suspicions I already had about the death of poor James Rushworth.'

On leaving the room we encountered one of the maids, who gave us an odd, sideways look. I thought perhaps she was shocked at seeing me emerge from a bedroom with Colonel Hartley but she turned and begged my pardon.

'Excuse me, miss – and you too, sir – but there's something I ought to tell you. It may seem ridiculous and I know you may not believe me but I swear it's true. You can ask

Thomas if you like – he didn't see quite what I saw but he saw *something*.'

'What did you see?'

'This morning, sir – a man dressed as a monk in a grey robe – he was gliding along the corridor. It's a bit dark along here and his back was towards me and that hood over his head so I didn't see his face. I won't say it was a ghost but I don't know who or what it was. I saw Thomas coming out of Sir Ralph's room so I called to him and we both went after him – or whatever it was – and he went into the Tapestry Room and Thomas went in and called me and there was no one there. The room was quite empty. I really did see something, sir.'

'I'm sure you did. Sarah, isn't it? You've worked here many years and I remember you were with old Miss Wilton.'

'Twelve years, sir. Yes, I was kept on by Sir Ralph and her ladyship.'

'Did you go in the closet?' I asked, remembering my own experience in the Tapestry Room.

'No, miss, it was locked. I'm not saying it was a ghost, but it was *somebody*!'

'I'm sure it was,' said Colonel Hartley. 'Come along, Miss Tyler, let's have a look at it now.'

We entered the Tapestry Room and as we expected, it was empty.

'Where's this closet you mentioned?'

'Here.' I held back the tapestry and showed him the hidden door in the panelling.

'I didn't know about this.' He tried the latch and the door opened easily. 'Sarah said it was locked,' he said.

'Yes, and that was strange because there is no lock – only

a bolt inside. Come and see.'

'So our mysterious monk could have slipped inside, shot the bolt and been safe from discovery?'

I then told him of the experience I had had in the early days of my visit to Lovegrove.

'I've always felt sure that the woman I heard was Louisa Thorpe but I wasn't at all certain about the man. I distinctly heard a male voice and a woman's but quite muffled. I couldn't make out any words. I've always feared the man might be my brother – she was quite blatant in her advances.'

'Yes, but I shouldn't be too sure of that.' He looked carefully around the small room. I could not see any difference in my surroundings but it could be that my recollection had faded. There was a candlestick and a small tinderbox that I could not remember but such items are easily disregarded.

'Did you open the chest and find a skeleton?' he smiled.

'Oh, I certainly looked but it seemed to contain nothing but old musty curtains and counterpanes.'

'Just as well you didn't enter and disturb the happy couple. You'd probably have had a nasty shock – though not nearly as nasty as that suffered by the guilty pair.'

'I think the door was bolted.'

'Certainly it was – they wouldn't want their assignation to be interrupted.'

He glanced around the room again and turned his attention to the daybed and peered at one of the crushed cushions. He picked it up and carried it to the window, calling me over to join him.

'Hold this,' he said, and I took the cushion in my arms. He carefully removed a long golden hair from the surface.

'Now, whose is this, I wonder.'

A pile of mildewed prayer books lay stacked in a corner of the room. I removed a blank page from the back of one and used it to enclose the hair, which he placed in his pocket.

'Someone has certainly been lying on here – sleeping, perhaps – or otherwise.' He sank to his knees and felt underneath the bed. 'I don't think the servants dust under here very often,' he added.

He then brought out a bottle of wine and a jug of water covered by a napkin and commented that neither looked as though it had been there very long.

'We'd better leave everything as we found it. I'd like a closer look at this chest.'

He attempted to raise the lid and I went to help him, thinking he could not easily lift it one-handed, but he shook his head.

'You say you looked inside?'

'Yes, there was a key in the keyhole but it wasn't locked.'

'Now it is and there's no key. I wonder what's hidden inside? I suppose we could get it forced open but that would give warning to whoever is using this room. Leave it for now, I've seen all I want to see. It's very hot and airless in here. Let's go.'

We returned to the Tapestry Room.

'Who do you suppose Sarah saw this morning?' I asked.

'Whoever it was had gone to search Mrs Thorpe's room. Someone who knew about the letter addressed to me – or at least, suspected something of the sort might exist. Someone who needed to clean the marble obelisk more thoroughly.'

'And he was dressed as a monk?'

'The hermit was provided with two robes. He died wearing

one but I shouldn't be surprised if the other is missing. I'll check his cell. It probably used to be kept in his trunk with his other clothes but I can't recall seeing it when we went through his things – can you?'

I shook my head. 'I suppose it would be a good disguise, especially with the hood pulled low to shade the face. And when Sarah and Thomas followed him into this bedroom he shut himself in the closet.'

'It seems like it. Quite a good hiding place as this room is never used.'

'And what about the so-called ghost that the other maid – the silly one – said she saw gliding into the priory ruins?'

'Oh, she certainly saw someone, though I'm not at all sure what he was doing out there.'

He put his hand on my shoulder. 'Charlotte ...' (It was only afterwards I realized he had called me by my Christian name for the first time.) 'Don't tell anyone of this, not even your brother. It seems to me this house hides one secret too many. Remember what I said before – take care!'

# CHAPTER TWENTY

The next twenty-four hours were full of upheavals and make-shift arrangements. The coroner returned with a hastily convened jury who inspected the scene of the accident and viewed the unfortunate corpse. By now, Louisa Thorpe was decently coffined and placed on the dining room table, where she could be discreetly glimpsed before being lidded but not screwed down, in case her next of kin wished to view her when they arrived.

The inquest was held first thing the following morning and proceeded with great rapidity, a verdict of 'accidental death' being brought in within the hour, much to everyone's relief.

Lady Denby had sent a trusted servant to take a letter to Morley Rectory in Cheshire to inform Mrs Lawrence of her sister's death and inviting her, with her husband the rector, to stay at Lovegrove until the sad obsequies were completed. She had decided against using the post as she wanted to ensure an immediate reply. This she received the next day from Mrs Lawrence, rather terse and formal compared with her ladyship's gushing effusion, saying she would be starting out immediately, but as her husband, the Revd Titus

Lawrence, was unable to leave his parish duties, she would be escorted by her son.

'Two rooms instead of one, how provoking!' cried Lady Denby. 'Rowland must be moved, though I'd hate to send him back to that hussy he's married.'

'Why not put Mrs Lawrence in her sister's room?' suggested Elinor.

'What? The room where she died?'

'She was already dead when she was taken back to her room – besides, lots of people sleep in rooms where their relatives died,' said Elinor. 'It can't stay empty forever and it's one of the best bedrooms in the house. There's the Tapestry Room, of course. . . .'

'The Tapestry Room? Oh no, not there – it's not at all comfortable. I suppose she *could* go in Louisa's room and her son in Rowland's but then, where do we put Rowland?'

'The Blue Room?'

'No, he might as well stay where he is and Mr Lawrence can have the Blue Room. It's very small but young men aren't usually all that fussy, especially if they've been away to school.'

That being settled, Mrs Thorpe's room and the Blue Room were prepared for the expected guests. We used the breakfast room for all our meals as the dining room was otherwise occupied and this proved perfectly adequate as our numbers were so much reduced. Sir Ralph, who had been hoping to come downstairs, decided to stay where he was so that he could avoid the visitors. He had decided they were 'not his sort.' He did, however, promise to attend the funeral at the parish church.

There was some debate as to whether Louisa's dead

husband's family should be invited but as Mr Thorpe had been thirty years older than his wife they were few and elderly and lived a hundred miles away. Lady Denby decided it was enough to write and inform them of Louisa's death. In any case the dead woman had not liked any of her in-laws, who strongly disapproved of Mr Thorpe's marriage. Louisa had deeply resented the fact that he had left them all his fortune. I wondered if there was a particular reason for this; perhaps he was aware of a certain tendency to disregard her marriage vows.

'If only Frank would return!' exclaimed Lady Denby. 'He was like a son to her. But we have no means of finding him in time. He said he was going away for a few days and then coming back. Suppose he returns on the day of the funeral? Poor boy – what a shock!'

No more apparitions were seen, though two of the maids reported mysterious footsteps being heard, creaking floorboards and the like. The cook complained of petty pilfering from the larder, but that happened occasionally and with so many people traipsing through the house there were bound to be irregularities.

Lady Denby had arrayed herself in deepest black, which I thought excessive as she was not related to the deceased, but her reaction to all the events of her life was nothing if not dramatic.

'All got up like the Tragic Muse,' said Elinor unsympathetically.

The local vicar, the Revd Amos Phillips, did not get on with the Denbys. At least, he would probably have got on well enough with Sir Ralph, but her ladyship was in charge of the household's religious welfare. I am not sure what her beliefs were but I am sure they were not conventional. Though she and her family attended the parish church fairly regularly, 'to set a good example', I fancy her taste ran to mysterious monks, renegade priests, walled-up nuns and sinister abbots rather than dull English vicars and curates.

Mr Phillips was elderly, scholarly, shy and retiring, as well as being extremely deaf. Rather than be bullied and hectored by Lady Denby he kept out of her way.

On this occasion, however, he felt obliged to visit the priory and offer his condolences to the family, at the same time discussing arrangements for the forthcoming funeral. Lady Denby asked me to be present during the interview.

'Do help me to talk to Mr Phillips, dear. He is so very hard of hearing and I find it so tedious to repeat things. We must make sure he has understood all the important details – the small talk doesn't matter.'

I thought he must be profoundly deaf indeed if her ladyship's booming voice did not penetrate his ears.

'I understand the unfortunate Mrs Thorpe was a friend of many years' standing,' he began gently.

'She was my friend from schooldays. Sir Ralph and the others didn't really know her.'

'Perhaps you can give me some idea of the arrangements required for the funeral,' he continued, 'though perhaps I ought to see Sir Ralph as he will be the chief mourner.'

I wondered for a moment if Lady Denby would insist on attending the funeral herself in defiance of custom but she did not go that far. Throwing flower petals and making orations at the hermit's interment were not the same as a proper funeral in church.

'Well, I'm not at all sure about that,' said Lady Denby.

'We are not related after all. He will certainly attend if he is well enough, with my son and perhaps Colonel Hartley, but I am awaiting the arrival of Mrs Thorpe's sister and her son – I'm not sure which one but the eldest, who was very close to his aunt, is in London and we are unable to contact him. I should point out—' She broke off abruptly.

'What's that?' she said, startled.

'What's what?' enquired Mr Phillips.

I had heard it too – a sharp crack like a shot from outside – then another.

Lady Denby rose and went to the window. 'How strange – two men are running towards the priory ruins. I think one of them is Colonel Hartley – yes, and the other is that man-servant of his – the one who was in the army with him!'

'Sam Bates? Then he must have returned!' I exclaimed, rising to join her.

'Returned from where? No, I can't see any more.'

'I'll find out what's going on,' I offered, glad of a chance to escape.

'No Miss Tyler, there's no need – I'm sure we'll hear about it soon enough. It may be dangerous. . . .'

But I excused myself and left the room. I went through the vestibule to the side door and stood looking in the direction of the priory ruins but I could see nothing, though I heard a few shouts. Presently I ventured out and almost collided with Sam Bates, who was running towards the house. He was red-faced and somewhat out of breath.

'Get back inside, miss! The Colonel would be very concerned if he knew you were here.'

'Why? What's happened? Where is he?'

'Let's get you indoors first, miss, and then I'll tell you.' He escorted me back into the vestibule.

'We heard something that sounded like shots,' I said, 'two shots – and saw Colonel Hartley and you running towards the ruins.'

'That's right, miss. Somebody took a shot at us from the old priory. It carried off the Colonel's hat and the second one missed him. We ran back before he had time to reload.'

'And suppose he had other firearms ready loaded?'

'We had to take that risk. We're used to being fired at but you don't expect it in an English park.'

'Thank God neither of you was hurt. But where *is* he?'

'We had a good look round but couldn't see anyone. Whoever fired the shots had vamoosed, as we used to say in Spain. The Colonel went back to find his hat.'

At that moment he came through the door, bareheaded with his hair even more tousled than usual and his face flushed, which showed up the scar more vividly. Yet his eyes were sparkling and his expression animated.

'You here!' he exclaimed. 'I hope you didn't venture out.'

'Not very far,' I admitted.

'Oh, you foolish girl, you could have been shot.'

'He'd already fired at you so I didn't think I was in much danger – and you were running about, trying to find him. Who was it? Have you any idea at all?'

'Someone who thinks I know too much. See here!' he held up his grey hat and showed me two bullet holes. 'Straight through, and too close for comfort. I can do without an arm but I'm not sure I could manage without a brain.'

If Bates had not been there I think I would have been tempted to throw my arms round his neck, so relieved was I at his escape and so anxious for his safety.

'Sam here found the gunsmith who sold a pair of officer's pistols to someone from this house. He had a record of the date, the cost and a brief description of the firearms in question. He also recognized the purchaser from one of your sketches. So this, and the letter from Mrs Thorpe, must have the villain worried. He's aware that I probably have enough evidence to have him arrested but not, I fear, to hang him.'

'But who?'

'Presently. All shall be revealed in the best traditions of drama. I think now, Bates, it might be safe enough to fetch our horses and see them stabled here for a while. I was coming to have a word with Sir Ralph and give an account of the latest developments,' he explained.

When Sam Bates had gone he held open the inner door for me, rather awkwardly as he was still holding his hat and was obliged to perch it on his head for a moment while he turned the handle. These occasional small stratagems and signs of clumsiness touched me to the heart, but seeing my expression he thought I was concerned for his hat.

'Ruined!' he said ruefully. 'And nearly new. If the holes were a bit lower I might have had them hidden by a wider ribbon. No consideration at all, our assailant.'

'You could have been killed.'

'Not for the first time in my life. Cheer up, my dear – but it was foolish of you to venture out of doors after you'd heard shots. Promise me you won't do anything like that again.'

'I hope the occasion won't arise. You must admit it doesn't happen very often.'

'And we'll keep quiet about this particular incident. We can make up some story to satisfy Lady Denby – I don't want to alarm anyone unnecessarily and I don't want to put the would-be assassin on his guard.'

'But you are the one in danger.'

'Which is something I'm well used to – as is Sam Bates. There's no need to involve anyone else at present – which is why I'd rather not tell you everything I know at this stage.'

As we entered the main entrance hall we heard a babble of voices and discovered two visitors had just arrived. Lady Denby was there with the vicar beside her and she was greeting a short, stout lady with a high complexion and dark hair streaked with grey. She was dressed in mourning and her face wore a dour expression. Despite being rather plain there was enough of a family resemblance for me to recognize Mrs Thorpe's sister. A young man stood beside her, obviously the son whom she had informed us would escort her and represent his parents at the funeral.

'We are so sorry Frank isn't here but I wondered if you knew where he might be contacted,' Lady Denby was saying.

'Frank?' Mrs Lawrence looked bewildered. 'Who is Frank?'

'Oh, of course, I believe you don't call him that. I know Frank likes his friends to use that name but his family probably don't. His real name is Frederick, I seem to recall.'

'I don't know who you are talking about.'

'Your son – your eldest son. I understood he was christened Frederick but liked to be called Frank. He was staying here with his Aunt Louisa but he left for London before she had that dreadful accident.'

'I still don't know what you mean. *This* is my eldest son Frederick.' She indicated the young man beside her. 'The person you are talking about must be an imposter.'

# CHAPTER TWENTY-ONE

All was astonishment and consternation. Only Colonel Hartley seemed not at all surprised.

'But who *is* this Frank?' demanded Lady Denby. 'And *why* was this deception practised on us?'

'I think you know,' I whispered to the Colonel.

'Yes,' he murmured, 'but I'm not going to blurt it out in front of this crowd. They'll get it half right, I'm sure.'

'I had a letter from Louisa,' said Mrs Lawrence, 'and in it she gave the impression that she was staying at Lovegrove on her own. My sister's morals were her own business but she knew I strongly disapproved of her liaisons. I can only conclude that this so-called Frank Lawrence, who stole our name in order to deceive you, was her latest lover.'

'But he must have been at least a dozen years younger,' protested Lady Denby.

'That made no difference to Louisa,' sniffed Mrs Lawrence. 'That's why we didn't get on – the more I criticized her behaviour the worse she became so in the end we had little to do with each other.'

'I feel really hurt by her duplicity,' complained her lady-ship. 'I know one shouldn't speak ill of the dead but really – I

feel *betrayed*! And as for that saucy, hypocritical young man
– words fail me!'

'Not for long,' whispered Colonel Hartley.

The guests were ushered into the library while their
luggage was taken upstairs. Mr Phillips was included in
the party as the funeral was still under discussion. That
left the two of us standing at the side of the entrance hall,
apparently unnoticed by either the newcomers or their
hostess.

'Can we find somewhere to talk?' asked the Colonel.

I led him into a little dark parlour, not much used, where
we were unlikely to be interrupted.

'I think I had better tell you all I know,' he said, when
we were comfortably settled. 'I have suspected for some time
that Frank Lawrence was not all he pretended to be. His
real name is Fortescue Rushworth.'

'Fortescue?' I burst out laughing.

'Yes, a silly name but commonplace in his family.'

'But Rushworth – that was the hermit's real name.'

'Yes – they were related – second cousins once removed. I
told you James Rushworth was heir to a considerable estate
in Devonshire when his uncle died. The old man, in failing
health, tried for months to trace him but died before he could
find out where he was. The next heir was our friend Frank,
who really did prefer to be called by that name, and who can
blame him?

'I wrote to the uncle after Rushworth's death, not knowing
the old man was no more. The family attorney read my letter
and then saw a report of the inquest in *The Times*. The
lawyer came to Ashdale as soon as he could.'

'That would be the man Rowland saw at the Unicorn,

asking questions about Lovegrove and mentioning you by name.'

'Yes, he came to see me. Of course, there was no proof that Frank Lawrence was really Frank Rushworth but it seemed obvious he had used his affair with Mrs Thorpe to gain admission to Lovegrove as an invited guest and take all the time he needed to kill the heir to the Devonshire estate. He could then go down to Devon and present himself as the next heir. There would be nothing to connect him with Lovegrove. Unfortunately for him he can't go there until he has destroyed any evidence against him. I could at least question his right to the property and that might instigate a more thorough probing into Rushworth's death.'

'But how did he find out who the hermit really was and where he was?'

'Somehow he managed to trace him to Manchester where he'd worked for several years as a tutor to a mill-owner's sickly son. He was using a false name, of course, but he had money banked under his real name. I'm not sure of the details yet but the Manchester people knew where he'd gone. Frank Rushworth made enquiries about Lovegrove and – again I don't know how – met Mrs Thorpe, who was only too eager to accept the advances of a handsome young man.'

'So it was those two I heard in the closet – I'm quite relieved – I feared it was my brother George.'

'I'm very glad it wasn't! Anyway he persuaded her – without much difficulty, I imagine – to bring him here in the guise of her nephew.'

'Do you think she knew of his plans to murder Brother Caspar?'

'I don't think so – at least, not at first. Mrs Thorpe may

have been promiscuous but however besotted she was with Frank I'm sure she would have drawn the line at aiding and abetting a murderer. She wrote me a letter—'

'The one she left in the writing-table?'

'Yes, she told me of her suspicions; she had seen the pistols in his room and wondered what he was about. He didn't confide in her but she managed to get some information out of him. She found out the connection with the Rushworths of Devon and guessed much of the rest. For all that, she wanted him to stay with her and when he took off for London she no longer trusted him and I think she warned him she was going to put her suspicions in writing to ensure his return.'

'Do you think she wanted him to marry her?'

'Oh yes, I think she was insisting on it once he came into his fortune. Your brother was a second string in case her plan failed.'

'You think she was murdered?'

'Probably. Frank certainly has an accomplice in this house and I'm not yet sure who it is.'

At that moment the door opened and my brother entered.

'Oh, there you are – I thought I heard voices. There seems quite a lot going on. Have you seen Sophie?'

'She's with Elinor,' I replied. 'They're in Sir Ralph's room, reading some comedy to him to amuse him.'

'They seem quite friendly now, those two. I thought at first they weren't going to get on.'

'I think Elinor decided Sophie wasn't just a silly fribble after all and Sophie decided Elinor was rather more than a bluestocking.'

'Ah well, I suppose they can amuse each other. What's going on? I understand Mrs Thorpe's sister has arrived.'

'Come and sit down and we'll tell you,' I said.

Between us the Colonel and I explained what had happened but nothing was said about Frank's real identity and
character.

'The unmitigated scoundrel!' exclaimed George, who
looked relieved rather than shocked. 'Now he's cleared off
before it all came to light. What a rogue! Mind you, it's not
quite as bad as I supposed.' As George still had no idea of
the depths of Frank Rushworth's villainy he could not be
referring to murder and mayhem.

'George,' I said, 'I think the time has come for you to tell
us what it was you saw concerning Mrs Thorpe. One day you
were flirting quite absurdly and the next you were calling
her depraved.'

'Ah well, that was when I thought Frank Lawrence was
her nephew. I went in the library and found them on the sofa
together, kissing and – er – rather more than kissing. They
were so absorbed in their activities that they didn't hear me
enter and I got out pretty quickly, I can tell you. I've never
been more embarrassed in my life. I thought she was having
an affair with her nephew and flirting with me to divert
attention from her real interest. It's still pretty bad – bringing a young lover to stay under the roof of her friend – but
it's not as bad as incest.'

I think Colonel Hartley and I tacitly decided not to tell
George the full story at this stage; he knew quite enough to
be going on with.

'He seemed such a pleasant fellow too,' said George won-
deringly. 'I liked him at first. This Mrs Lawrence must be
very upset, especially as she's got her son with her – the very
man who was being impersonated.'

'I think Mrs Lawrence is capable of dealing with any circumstances and her son seems to be a serious, sober young man,' I said. 'I don't think they'll be unduly distressed.'

This proved to be the case. Colonel Hartley was invited to stay for dinner and it was a solemn meal. Mrs Lawrence was a dour, sarcastic woman who was not at all impressed by Lady Denby's histrionics. Her son said little, partly through shyness, I thought, but also on account of a tendency to observe rather than participate. He was obviously intelligent and once or twice I caught a trace of sardonic humour. He seemed rather taken with Elinor and was certainly impressed later in the evening with her skill on the piano.

'I'm not sure music is appropriate in a house of mourning,' said Mrs Lawrence, determined not to enjoy anything.

'It's very serious music,' declared Lady Denby.

'I see nothing wrong,' said Frederick Lawrence, 'providing there is no frivolity. Serious music can create a suitably solemn and contemplative atmosphere.'

'Oh well, if you say so,' his mother conceded.

It would otherwise have been difficult to entertain the Lawrences as conversation was stilted and awkward. Without Colonel Hartley beside me I would have been extremely bored. Even if we sat in silence it was enough for me.

'Of course,' Mrs Lawrence observed, 'Louisa was ten and away at school when I married. We were never close as I was the eldest and there were three other girls in between. She was never like the rest of us – always wild and wilful, even as a child.'

'Oh yes, she was often in trouble at school,' recalled Lady Denby. 'I remember she was caught dropping notes from the window to a handsome young gardener who was tending the grounds. I'm not at all sure he could read but she was quite unrepentant. It was a harmless, girlish prank after all. She was so full of life.'

Lady Denby dabbed her eyes. 'I can't believe I'll never hear her laugh again. And that she should die under my roof – in such tragic circumstances! A terrible shock to us all!'

'I'm sure it was,' said Mrs Lawrence, 'especially as you recently had a suicide on the premises – or so Louisa stated in her letter.'

'Ah, that was our hermit – poor man! It wasn't in the house, of course – he had a cave with an adjoining cell in the grounds near the lake to the rear.'

'He was rather more than a hermit,' said Colonel Hartley quietly.

'Of course,' Lady Denby conceded, 'he was your friend, wasn't he?'

'Friends with a hermit?' Mrs Lawrence seemed puzzled. 'I've heard about people keeping hermits but I thought they were old vagrants or something of that sort.'

'Not this one. He was a gallant officer who wished to retire from the world,' the Colonel informed her.

'Really? There is no accounting for tastes.'

'The trouble is,' Lady Denby continued, dragging the conversation back to its original subject, 'we don't know how Louisa came to meet this Frank person. He seemed quite gentlemanlike in appearance and manner – well educated and good-looking.'

'He would be!' Mrs Lawrence said derisively. 'Louisa moved in different circles from me. She liked to mix with rather rackety people – the sort who gamble and go to horse races and dance all night. Not *our* sort at all. She could have met him anywhere.'

'That's the problem. We thought you would know where he was but he's turned out to be a complete stranger. Even so, I suppose he ought to know what's happened.'

'I don't see why.' Mrs Lawrence looked disapproving. 'He was obviously a rogue and a deceiver. By now he's probably found some other unfortunate woman to tangle in his wiles.'

I thought it only too likely and remembered how once, in the early days of our acquaintance, I too had been attracted by his charm.

# CHAPTER TWENTY-TWO

The next morning the funeral took place. Colonel Hartley suggested that I should escort Sophie and Elinor to Shelbourne where we could stay for luncheon and return to Lovegrove for dinner. I was delighted with the idea and so were the girls, who were relieved to escape from the gloom surrounding Mrs Thorpe's obsequies.

Lady Denby and Mrs Lawrence, assisted by Louisa's maid, were to spend the morning packing her belongings.

Sir Ralph, who had been coming downstairs for a few hours every day, said he felt well enough to attend the church. Frederick Lawrence, Rowland and George accompanied him. My brother was rather embarrassed by the whole procedure but felt it was his duty to attend.

'After all,' he said, 'I was one of the last friends she had. She was more to be pitied than reviled and there are few enough going to be present.'

Colonel Hartley had decided that as he scarcely knew Mrs Thorpe, he was not obliged to put in an appearance; but to please the Denbys he sent an empty carriage as a mark of respect.

As it was a fine morning and the distance barely a mile

I decided we would walk. The Colonel had promised to send us back in his carriage, which by then would have returned from the funeral.

'Coming here is like going from night to day,' said Elinor, 'though the house needs a woman's touch.'

I knew what she meant; the house was bright, comfortable and orderly but rather shabby and masculine. There were many portraits of officers in redcoats, hanging swords and paintings of battle scenes, and the like, but mercifully none of the ancient weaponry that bedecked Lovegrove Priory. Old General Hartley was in a wheeled chair but as charming and kindly as ever in his bluff, outspoken way. He was very proud of his garden and had himself pushed around by a manservant to show us his favourite flowers and trees. We were followed by several large dogs.

At one point, the girls were inspecting a fountain full of goldfish and the manservant had gone over to explain how the flow of water was controlled. The old general suddenly seized my hand.

'My dear, don't take this amiss but this place needs a mistress – a young lady like you. John thinks very highly of you – I'm sure you know that.'

I felt my cheeks burning. 'He hasn't said anything – why should he? We've only known each other a few weeks.'

'Quite long enough! I want you to know I'd be more than happy for you to be my daughter.'

I scarcely knew what to say. 'That's very kind of you but things must take their course. I'll be going home soon and I don't know when – or even if – I'll ever come again. Our visit hasn't been an overwhelming success. I believe Lady Denby had some idea of making a match between Rowland

and Sophie but of course that came to nothing.'

'I hope Sophie wasn't disappointed. That boy's a useless lump anyway.'

'Not at all. She's in no hurry to marry and I'm sure she'll do better if she waits a few years.'

'Of course she will! And that girl Elinor – I've always felt sorry for her. Sir Ralph's a good enough fellow but that dreadful wife of his – excuse me, I'm too outspoken, I know you are kin.'

'I think most people would agree with you. As for being related, it is quite a distant connection and I'd never met her before this visit. My brother George last saw her when he was twelve. Apart from an occasional letter, we've never had much to do with each other.'

'That's a relief! I once tried to read one of her novels but I couldn't get on with it at all – nothing but gloomy castles and girls swooning. I'm sure you're not the sort of girl who goes in for swooning.'

'Well, I must admit I've never done it.'

'I should think not! Anyway, I prefer something like *Tom Jones* or *Humphry Clinker.*'

I laughed. 'So do I – but I have read her ladyship's novels and Sophie used to be very fond of them. Since meeting Lady Denby I think she's changed her mind.'

'And who can blame her? Ah, here comes John – he's obviously finished with the bailiff. Now I'm going indoors and he can take over. I'm sure you prefer his company to mine.'

'Not at all, I think we get on very well.'

'So we do – and remember what I said.' With that he summoned his servant and was wheeled back to the house.

'I hope my father hasn't been boring you,' said Colonel

Hartley. 'He doesn't often have the opportunity of talking to ladies and he does enjoy their company.'

'Well, I enjoy his and he's not at all boring. I agree with him on most things.'

'He can be rather blunt and dogmatic at times – perhaps it's the privilege of age and high military rank.'

'I like him immensely and he seems to like me.'

'Oh he does – and that's hardly surprising. Are the dogs bothering you?'

'Of course not – we have several at home and I'm missing them.'

'Yes, I expect you'll be glad to go.'

'Not entirely. This part of the country has great attractions.'

'I'm glad you think so.' Then the girls ran to join us and we could say no more.

'I think you ought to marry Colonel Hartley,' said Sophie as we drove back to Lovegrove in his carriage, newly returned from its funeral duties. 'It would be nice to come and stay with you here and I'm sure you'd work wonders on the house. The curtains are faded and the carpets worn and I really think they can't *see* it. Men are like that, aren't they? Papa's the same – he'd never replace anything if it wasn't for you.'

'But I really can't marry someone just to oblige you,' I said lightly, 'despite the need for new furnishings. A draper might do as much for them.'

'You know what I mean,' said Sophie.

'Do I? Perhaps we'd better concentrate on the immediate future. Do you think your papa will be well enough to leave now, Elinor? If he's managed to attend the funeral he should be almost back to normal.'

'I hope so. I want to see how he has borne it. The ceremony must have been quite a strain after several days of doing very little.'

'I'm sure Lady Denby will make him rest. I really do think she is very fond of him, Elinor.'

'Yes, I suppose so but her affection doesn't extend to me. If anything happened to Papa my life wouldn't be worth living.'

'Oh, don't say that!' cried Sophie. 'Life is always worth living.'

'For you, perhaps, with a kind father and aunt and a pleasant home where you truly belong. I was happy enough before my father married again. I don't know what would happen to me if I was left alone in the world.'

'You would at least be well provided for,' I said, 'and when you are of age you could perhaps hire a respectable companion and enjoy a little independence – travel, perhaps – indulge your taste for music.'

She brightened visibly. I do not think the idea had occurred to her except as a fantasy.

Sir Ralph had, indeed, survived the morning's ordeal remarkably well. He had lost a little weight during the previous week but had regained his usual healthy colour and seemed quite lively again. His wife fussed over him to excess but he bore it cheerfully enough now he felt so much better.

There was, perhaps, a certain relief that the funeral was over. Mrs Lawrence received an account of the proceedings from her son.

'I suppose it was all very well,' she said, 'but I little thought my sister would lie in a strange churchyard with so few friends to attend her laying to rest.'

'But she never liked living in her cottage, by all accounts,' said Frederick. 'She was always visiting somewhere else and she had no connections with her local church – I don't think she attended very often.'

'Then I suppose we must be content. As things have turned out her death was so sudden there was little we could do about it.'

'Tomorrow morning I'll show you the grave,' her son promised. 'It should be filled in by then and I've ordered a simple wooden marker until we have a proper headstone made.'

'And then there's the trouble of her estate, such as it is,' Mrs Lawrence continued. 'I presume she left a will. The cottage was rented but she had a small amount of money – about two hundred a year in the Funds, I seem to remember. She had to sell most of her jewellery.'

'Her attorney will probably have her will if she made one – some people don't – in which case you and your sisters would inherit. If the money was an annuity it would end with her death.'

'One thing,' said Rowland cheerfully, 'no one would have pushed her downstairs to claim her fortune.'

Everyone stared at him in silence. Mrs Lawrence glared. Lady Denby hastened to cover up her son's crass lack of tact and he began to realize he had offended. He excused himself and left the room. A little later I caught sight of him through the window riding towards the gates. I presumed he was going to join his beloved Carrie in their lodgings in Ashdale.

Dinner was again a sober affair, especially as everyone was aware of its being eaten off the table on which Louisa Thorpe's coffin had rested until that morning.

The Lawrences had declared their intention of visiting

the churchyard and attending matins as it was a Sunday and they disapproved of travelling on that day. On Monday they were to leave early for Cheshire. Lady Denby protested and tried to persuade them to stay longer but I thought her entreaties half-hearted and insincere. They reminded her too forcibly of the recent tragedy and she had nothing in common with Mrs Lawrence, who had not even heard of her novels and was far too perspicacious to be impressed by her extravagant posturing.

When I retired that night I reflected what an odd day it had been. The morning and the afternoon seemed to belong to different worlds; one a garden full of sunlight and promise for the future, the other an evening of solemnity and awkwardness and a generally disagreeable atmosphere.

The day after tomorrow, George had decided, we would travel home. I was longing to leave Lovegrove but felt I could hardly bear the parting that would ensue. Perhaps it was my fate to be always parted from what I loved most.

# CHAPTER TWENTY-THREE

The next morning, Mrs Lawrence and her son walked the half-mile to the village church to have a look at Louisa Thorpe's grave. Lady Denby insisted on accompanying them though I am sure they would have preferred to go alone. As it was Sunday they intended to attend the morning service and Lady Denby, who was by no means a regular member of the congregation, decided it was her duty to be present. Sophie and I saw them leave as we returned from our morning walk.

As we approached the house one of the maids came out to meet us. I recognized Susan, the servant who had claimed to see the hermit's ghost and threw a fit of hysterics in the entrance hall.

'Please, miss, could I have a word with you alone?' she asked, somewhat anxiously, and would say no more until Sophie had gone back into the house.

'It's Colonel Hartley, miss; he came here while you were on your walk and he wants to see you urgently. He says to tell you he wants to see you in the Tapestry Room closet and that he's discovered something there that he thinks you ought to see.' She spoke carefully and then looked pleased with herself, as if struggling to remember the exact words and feeling satisfied at having managed it. A nice enough girl, I thought, but not very intelligent and not likely to rise very high in the ranks of the servants' hall.

'Thank you, Susan, you may go.' She ran off as though glad to escape. Delivering messages was probably an ordeal for her.

I hastened into the house and upstairs to the Tapestry Room, which was now empty. Guessing that the Colonel was already in the closet as the door stood slightly ajar, I pushed it open.

'I thought you couldn't wait to get here. Quite besotted with him, aren't you?'

I found myself face to face with Frank Lawrence, who was holding a pistol alarmingly close to my head. For a few seconds I felt my knees weaken but managed to overcome fear with anger.

'How dare you threaten me – you cheap little imposter. What are you doing here? I thought you were supposed to be in London.'

'I took the mail coach, travelled ten miles and then came back after dark. This is a very good hiding place – no one ever comes here, which is why Louisa Thorpe and I used it sometimes.'

'I heard you once.'

'Really? Louisa was always inclined to make a noise. Too much noise sometimes – she knew more than she ought and couldn't keep it to herself. But I haven't gone to all this trouble and made all these plans only to have interfering busybodies spoil it all. Sit down!'

I did not move and he suddenly seized me by the throat

and pressed the muzzle of the pistol to my temple. This time I was truly terrified; I had no doubt he would kill me if provoked too far. He forced me into a chair and tied my hands behind me with a length of cord.

'Screaming won't help – no one will hear. If I thought they would I'd gag you. Your lover will be here shortly, never fear.'

'He's not my lover.'

'Not for want of hoping, I imagine. Still, 'Armless 'Artley should be easy enough to manage considering his incapacity. I've only got to threaten to harm you and he'll do as I say. That's why I need the two of you. First of all I didn't know how much he'd told you and then, I knew he'd risk his own life – he's done it often enough before – but he won't risk yours.'

The little room was stifling and I began to feel a trifle faint. I remembered what the old General had said yesterday about my being unlikely to swoon. *Only* yesterday! Already it seemed a long way off.

'That Susan is obviously your little helper,' I said. 'Did you have to seduce her first?'

'She succumbed remarkably quickly – those sorts of girls always do. Pretty enough but no brain. Ever so eager to run little errands for me – to bring me food and drink, carry messages and so forth. She's used to clumsy pawing from enamoured footmen and grooms so a little finesse makes no end of an impression.'

'I imagine you told her to start a rumour about the hermit's ghost.'

'Yes, I had to coach her, of course, but I believe she did it rather well. The hermit's spare robe has been very useful – an excellent disguise and likely to add to rumours of a

191

phantom monk.

'Once I have disposed of you and your friend I shall be off to Devon to claim my inheritance. There will then be nothing to stand in my way – nothing *proved* anyway.'

'It's strange,' I said, anxious to keep him talking. 'I actually liked you at first.'

'Well, I liked you – still do, as a matter of fact. I had to show an interest in one of the females of the party to detract from Louisa. At first I thought of Sophie but Rowland had collared her. Elinor's too plain and prickly but you are pretty and clever – an irresistible combination. Pity you're so attracted by the military or our flirtation might have led to something really enjoyable.'

'It was never a flirtation and it couldn't have led anywhere.'

'Perhaps not, but poor Louisa had to be dealt with first; she had begun to get very tiresome and demanding even before she started asking awkward questions. She actually thought I'd marry her when I'd inherited my fortune – a penniless widow fifteen years my senior and rather silly and empty-headed to boot! I've lived on my wits for most of my life and I wasn't going to fall for *that*.'

'But was it necessary to kill the poor woman?'

'Of course it was. I could have shut her up by marrying her but that was never what I had in mind. She was beginning to disgust me.'

He stopped suddenly. I had heard it too: the faint creak of the Tapestry Room door opening and closing. He slipped behind my chair, put his arm across my throat and held the pistol to my head.

'Not a word!' he hissed.

The door opened and a voice spoke my name. Colonel Hartley's face changed in an instant from pleased anticipation to shock and horror. He summed up the situation in a few seconds.

'Let her go,' he said quietly. 'Let her go and you can do what you like with me.'

'The age of chivalry is not dead!' exclaimed Frank Lawrence mockingly. 'Why should I do that when I can do what I like with both of you?'

'Are you all right, Charlotte? Has he hurt you in any way?'

'No – don't worry about me.'

'What sweet concern for each other! A pity you won't live long enough to enjoy the consequences.'

'What are you going to do with us?' Colonel Hartley was remarkably calm as though he was asking the time of day.

'Oh, you'll soon find out. Everything is in readiness. I'm not attempting to mimic suicide or accident this time. You'll simply disappear.'

'Both of us?'

'Oh yes – I'll let you die together so you can enjoy your last moments in each others' arms – all three of them. Actually it will be a great deal longer than moments – rather drawn-out and unpleasant but you can comfort each other, I'm sure.'

'But you can't possibly kill two more people and escape scot-free,' I said, wondering desperately what he had in store for us. 'People will search – there'll be a great hue and cry.'

'By which time I'll be miles away. And it may be thought you've run away together – to Gretna Green, perhaps.'

'Why on earth would we do that?' asked Colonel Hartley. 'If we wanted to marry we could do it in the usual way with everyone's approval, I've no doubt.'

'I don't really care. No one knows I'm here except that stupid Susan and I may take her with me to keep her quiet. It would be quite a good subterfuge and I can always get rid of her later. Now, I'm getting rather tired of this pointless dialogue.' He loosened his grip and backed away, still holding the pistol aimed at me.

'Stand behind her,' he ordered, 'and put your hand on her shoulder where I can see.'

The Colonel stepped behind my chair and I felt the warm, firm clasp of his hand and was at once reassured. Frank backed towards an open trapdoor, kicking a stool out of the way. I realized then what it was. The heavy chest had been moved aside to reveal a small aperture in the floor.

'Behold – the second priest-hole!' declared Frank, with something very like glee. 'People have been searching for this for centuries so they're not likely to find it now. Louisa and I discovered it by accident when we tried to move the bed because she complained of a draught from the window.

'Now, untie the lady's hands, if you please, and we'll find her a suitable little lodging. That's right – don't try any foolish tricks, Colonel, or her life will end even more speed-ily than I had planned and you'll find yourself buried with a corpse. Almost like one of her ladyship's novels.

'Miss Tyler – or may I call you Charlotte? Come over here to this hole in the floor. You will find a ladder just inside. Climb down and stand below. There's not much room, I'm afraid, but it will just accommodate two at a pinch, though your companion *is* rather large.' For a few seconds his atten-tion was focused entirely on me as I followed his instructions and I heard a movement across the room.

'Don't try anything – I warned you!' snapped Frank.

A pair of long legs in riding boots and breeches began to descend the steps. The light from above was obliterated. Then there was a sudden scuffle as Colonel Hartley seized Frank's ankle and yanked it hard. There was the sound of a body sprawling and then a blow. The Colonel slid down the last few rungs and the trapdoor closed above us with a slam. There was a heavy grating noise and we were in total darkness.

# CHAPTER TWENTY-FOUR

'What happened? Did he hit you?' I put out my hands and found his shoulder.

'Yes, with the pistol butt – only a glancing blow but my face is rather painful so don't touch it. Come here, my poor girl, I should never have let you get involved in this.' He held me close and felt me trembling.

'Try to keep calm,' he said. 'Let us stand here quietly until we feel a little better. The worst thing we can do is panic. We'll wait until we are quite sure he has gone then we'll try to escape.'

'How?' my voice was faint and wavering.

'There's a way in so there's a way out. Lean on me until you feel stronger.'

'I'm not at all sure leaning on you has that effect,' I said after a short interval.

He managed to chuckle. 'Well, it's working wonders for me anyway.'

He rested his chin lightly on the top of my head and I closed my eyes. I thought that if only I wasn't so frightened and we were anywhere else at all I would think this was heaven.

'We'll stay quiet and listen,' he said, but we could hear nothing. It was very close and airless in the priest-hole and I wondered how long a man had been able to survive there.

'I feel sure he's gone,' he said at last, 'and I think we can have a little light on the proceedings before we try to get out. While Frank was putting you down here I managed to grab his tinderbox and a stump of a candle. We'll both feel better when we can see our surroundings. You'll have to strike the light, I'm afraid. It's one of the things I can no longer accomplish.'

My hands were still shaking so much I had difficulty striking the flint and igniting the tinder, though he held the box for me and encouraged my efforts. At last we had the candle lit and looked round. There was barely enough room for us to stand upright.

'Where exactly are we?' I wondered.

'Inside the outer wall of the house.' He climbed the ladder and put his shoulder to the trapdoor. After several attempts that made him grunt with effort, he confessed he could lift the trapdoor no more than a fraction of an inch.

'The blackguard has pushed the chest on top of us. I might have known!' For the first time I heard despair in his voice.

'How long can we survive without air?' I asked, rather tremulously.

'Don't think about it.'

I looked round frantically at the walls, which all seemed to be quite solidly made of ancient brick. Then I suddenly remembered something Sophie had said – long ago, it seemed, when we first came to Lovegrove. It was the day it had rained and I had first explored the Tapestry Room and discovered the closet. I had encountered Sophie and Rowland shortly afterwards; they had been tapping the panelling around the house, searching for the second priest-hole.

'There's supposed to be a passage leading from the hiding place to the priory ruins,' she had said. It was a tradition, a legend, no more, yet it did give a shred of hope.

'What are you doing?' he enquired.

I was holding the candle flame close to the walls, inspecting every inch. I told him what Sophie had said. 'It's at least worth looking,' I said.

'I wish you'd call me John,' he said suddenly. 'In these circumstances formality is ridiculous. Besides, we've just been a good deal closer than some married couples.'

'I'll call you anything you like if we can only get out of here. Look at this wall – doesn't something appear odd?'

He was standing close behind me and he peered over my shoulder. 'Why is it whitewashed? The other walls aren't – though it's a very old, dirty whitewash.'

It was indeed festooned with cobwebs and dust, but here and there was a break and grey filaments dangled in a ragged fringe where they had been torn. I knocked at the wall with my knuckles and hurt myself on rough bricks – which suddenly became smoother and gave out a loud rapping sound.

'I think there's a door,' I speculated, 'and the wood has been carved in a pattern of bricks and then everything whitewashed over.'

'It's been opened recently if those torn cobwebs are anything to go by. See if you can find some sort of handle.'

Nothing of the sort was visible but I discovered a small hole bored in the door. It was enough for me to gain a hold with two fingers and I pulled hard. There *was* a door and it opened more easily than I expected. A blast of air – dank and earthy – came to meet us. It was not fresh air by any means but it was a good deal better than what we had been breathing in the priest-hole.

'There are steps,' I said, peering down, 'very steep – more like a ladder than a staircase. Do you suppose Frank has been coming and going this way?'

'It seems likely – but let me squeeze past you and I'll go down first if you'll hold the candle.'

I shielded the flame with my hand, wondering what on earth I would do if it went out and I had to use the tinderbox again in pitch darkness. Colonel Hartley began to descend the steps.

'It's quite safe,' he said. 'If Frank Lawrence has been using it then it should be secure enough. You'd better keep the candle – I can't hold it and hang on to the steps. There's no rail so come down carefully.'

Despite the discomfort, and indeed the danger of our descent, we were both buoyed up by the hope of escape. I was hampered by my skirt, which was brushing against my poor companion's face, so I hitched it up to my knees and tucked it into my sash.

We reached the ground at last and found ourselves in a vaulted passageway. I hastily loosened my skirt until it fell to my feet again. I thought I heard him murmur 'Pity!' but I could have been mistaken.

'Only one way to go and that's forward,' he said. He took the candle from me and led the way.

'How far is it from the house to the priory ruins?' I asked. 'About a hundred yards, do you think?'

'Near enough and – damn – what's this?' He stumbled and nearly dropped the light.

'A white cloth under my feet – can you pick it up?'

I retrieved the object, which proved to be a lace-edged pillowcase stained with blood.

'Louisa Thorpe's pillowcase!' I exclaimed. 'He must have wrapped it round her head, as you surmised, to prevent the bloodstains before he threw her down the stairs – then he got rid of it down here.'

'Leave it for now; it can always be retrieved later if necessary. Let's get out of here first.'

We hurried on and suddenly emerged in a vaulted underground chamber supported by heavy pillars. In the centre stood a coffin, a brand new coffin with brass plate and handles.

'This must be right under the nave of the old priory church,' I said, 'so there are flagstones over our heads. How do we escape?'

'There may be some sort of exit but I doubt it. We'd better look first and if we don't find anything I'll try and shift one of those flagstones. They were removed very recently so they shouldn't be too difficult to raise.'

We were still prisoners but at least we had the hope of getting out. Above the paving which formed our roof was the sky and there were faint lines of daylight gleaming through the chinks in the stones. We searched the walls and found only a bricked-up archway which must once have led to another passage; then we again turned our attention to the coffin.

'I'm sorry, my poor friend, but you'll have to help us,' said John Hartley, climbing on the coffin lid and putting his shoulder to one of the flagstones above his head. This time his efforts yielded almost immediate results. The stone grated and rumbled a little and then slid aside, letting in a glorious burst of sunlight, fresh air and birdsong.

'I'm not at all sure I can get out,' he said. 'One really needs two arms – but you certainly can. Climb up here, put your hands on the edge of the aperture and I'll heave you up from below as best I can.'

It was a struggle but I was light and agile and managed at last to scramble out. I sat for a few moments, looking down at him. His hair was wildly tousled, there was a horrible swollen contusion on his left cheekbone which distorted the scar further and he was very dirty.

I looked at my torn and filthy dress, my blackened shoes and tattered stockings; my hair was falling down my back in wild disorder and I suddenly burst out laughing, perhaps in hysterical relief.

'What a pair we must look!' I gasped. ' I suppose we must go back to the house like this.'

'You'd better fetch help, I'm not high enough to get myself out and you can't help me on your own. See if you can find Sam Bates – he came with me when I got your note – except it wasn't from you. Frank Lawrence must have written it but it was very convincing and after all, I've never seen your handwriting.'

'Haven't you? No, of course you haven't. I suppose it was similar to the message I got saying you wanted to see me in the Tapestry Room closet as you'd found something of great significance.'

'He was taking a risk, of course – he didn't know that I hadn't seen your writing.'

'But Frank had – enough for him to do a reasonable forgery at least.' I hesitated. 'I don't want to leave you.'

'Then kiss me first.'

I crawled to the edge of the gap in the stones and leaned over. Our lips met briefly and then he seized me by the back of my head and kissed me again with a great deal more feeling.

'I like you with your hair down,' he said. 'Now *run!*'

# CHAPTER TWENTY-FIVE

I fled back to the house and at once encountered Lady Denby with the Lawrences, who had returned from their visit to the village church. They stared at me in amazement.

'Miss Tyler!' exclaimed her ladyship. 'What on earth has happened to you? Have you met with an accident?'

'You could say that. Mr Lawrence, could you go to the priory church where Colonel Hartley needs assistance? I must find his manservant.'

He took off immediately and without offering any explanations I ran on into the entrance hall where I found Sophie talking to Sam Bates.

'The very man!' I cried. 'The Colonel needs you at the priory church. I've already sent Mr Lawrence but I doubt if he can manage on his own. You may need a ladder – he's in the vault.'

Sam Bates did not linger to ask questions but ran outside to find his master.

'Aunt Charlotte!' shrieked Sophie. 'What an earth have you been doing? I'm so relieved to see you!' She hugged me wildly, not caring that some of the dirt and cobwebs transferred themselves to her white muslin gown.

'We've been looking for you,' she continued. 'At least *I* was looking for you and couldn't find you anywhere. Then I sent for that maid, Susan, who brought you a message. There was something odd about her manner – something sly and furtive. She told me some silly story about Sir Ralph wanting you to fetch him something from the gallery but I didn't believe a word of it. She asked to be excused but I said she wasn't to go until she told me the truth. I was sure something suspicious was going on.'

'It was indeed! That was very astute of you.'

'Aunt Charlotte, do you remember once telling me that there was nothing more despicable than striking a servant?'

'You didn't hit her?'

'No – but Elinor did. She came charging into the hall and demanded to know what was going on. I told her Susan knew something of your whereabouts but wouldn't tell. "Oh, yes she will!" said Elinor and struck her a swingeing blow across the face. The girl burst into tears – I almost felt sorry for her – and sobbed and cried and sank to the floor, but Elinor stood over her, yanked her head up by the hair and demanded to hear the whole story. She said she'd had to take a message to you to meet Colonel Hartley in the Tapestry Room. I asked her who told her to take the message but she wouldn't say.'

'Oh, I know who was responsible – Frank Lawrence. I suppose we still need to call him by that name until his real identity is known to everyone.'

'But he's in London!'

'No, he isn't – he's here and that accounts for the state I'm in. I'll tell you all about it when I have time but we must find Frank Lawrence – he tried to kill us.'

'Us?'

'Colonel Hartley and me.'

At that moment the Colonel entered with Sam Bates and Sophie gave a cry of horror.

'You look as though you've been buried alive,' she gasped.

'We very nearly were.'

'He looked worse after Waterloo,' added Sam Bates with a grin.

'I've been telling her about Frank Lawrence,' I said. 'The whole household must be warned.'

'That's what I'm about to do,' declared Colonel Hartley. 'He's extremely dangerous and armed. He may have already made his escape but I think there are too many people about the park to risk getting away by daylight. The Lawrences haven't seen anyone but that doesn't mean much as there are plenty of trees to provide cover. However, I think he's more likely to wait for darkness and then take a horse from the stable and ride off into the night.'

'What shall we do?' asked Sophie.

'The ladies must lie low until the men have searched the premises. See what firearms are in the house, Sam, and see the menservants are armed. I've left instructions for the gardeners and stablehands to comb the grounds. We must make a start at once.'

'I've brought one of our pistols, sir,' said Bates, 'ever since this trouble started.'

'You'd better come up to your room and change,' said Sophie. 'I'll send for Betsey and hot water.'

'Before I do I want to see that silly little Susan Brown,' I said. 'Where is she?'

'Still being bullied by Elinor, I suppose – she's called up the housekeeper as reinforcement.'

I exchanged a glance with John Hartley – the warmest and most understanding of looks – before he was off with Sam Bates to recruit his little regiment and give it instructions. Sophie led me into the Great Hall, where Susan Brown sat on a chair, her flushed, tear-stained face the very image of woe. Elinor stood over her in a threatening manner and Mrs Prosser, the housekeeper, jangled her keys and looked disapproving.

'There you are!' I cried. 'You silly girl – look at the state of me! Colonel Hartley and I were nearly killed as a result of your wicked deception.'

She at once burst into tears. More gently I asked her age but could not hear her mumbled reply.

'She's sixteen, Miss Tyler,' said the housekeeper.

'Only sixteen – and see what a mess you've got yourself into,' I continued. 'Your youth and ignorance excuse you to some extent, I suppose, but you need to know the truth. I know Frank Lawrence – and that's *not* his real name – is handsome and clever and has told you all sorts of lies. I suppose he's promised to take you with him?'

She nodded dumbly.

'I shouldn't count on it. I heard him say that if he *did* decide to take you he'd get rid of you later. I don't suppose he intends to murder you, though he's quite capable of that, but I imagine he'd simply abandon you in London or some other city where you'd be penniless and friendless. I'm sure even you know what happens to girls in such circumstances?'

The sobs grew louder until Elinor threatened to slap her again if she didn't quieten down.

'Where is he now – do you know?'

She shook her head. 'I was to wait for him after dark by

the hermit's cave.'

'You'd probably have waited all night. He's a bad man, Susan, and you must have nothing to do with him. He's responsible for two deaths and it could have been two more.'

I turned to the housekeeper. 'What will become of her?'

'Dismissed without a reference. We can't have a little cheat like that working here – and she's the one who stole from the larder, presumably to feed that nasty Mr Lawrence. I don't know his real name.'

'It seems a little harsh. I don't think she's really bad, merely foolish and misguided. Has she a family?'

'Her parents live in Creswood – that's about three miles from here.'

'Perhaps she could be paid a month's wages and sent back to them, saying she was unsuitable for domestic service. She might do better as a dairymaid or something of that sort.'

'I wish I'd never come here,' muttered the unfortunate Susan.

'So do we all!' cried Elinor. 'Really, Miss Tyler – what this wicked girl has made you suffer—'

'That's all over now. We must concentrate on finding Frank Lawrence. Did you know his real baptismal name was Fortescue?'

Elinor gave a hoot of laughter. 'Really? No wonder he changed it!'

The housekeeper marched Susan away to pack her few things and begin the dismal walk to her home village.

'Betsey's taken the hot water up for you,' announced Sophie from the doorway.

'Yes, I'll be glad to get rid of these clothes and wash off the grime.'

'Colonel Hartley doesn't seem to be bothering.'

'He's too intent on finding Frank Lawrence before he can do any more damage,' I said. 'Besides, they can get very dirty on the battlefield – gunsmoke and mud or dust – so I suppose he's used to it.'

I changed quickly when I got to my room and managed to wash off the worst of the filth though my hair was still in a sorry state.

'Never mind, miss,' said Betsey, helping me into clean clothes, 'you really need to have a proper bath and wash your hair but it will have to wait. I was lucky to get any hot water at all. The whole house is topsy-turvy at the moment – everyone running about and no one's where they're supposed to be.'

When I went downstairs again not a soul was in sight. I could hear distant voices and banging doors but there was no indication of what was going on. Sophie had followed me down.

'What shall we do? Perhaps you ought to rest,' she said, eyeing me doubtfully.

'Certainly not! I'm not an old woman, Sophie, and I could no more rest than I could fly in the air.'

'Look!' she cried. 'There's that telescope lying on the table – the one that Elinor used that first day when we went up on the roof. Why don't we go up there again? It's a shame to stay indoors but we can't very well go for another walk. The housekeeper said a cold luncheon had been set out in the dining room so we could help ourselves. Suppose I collect something for us to eat and we'll have a picnic on the roof away from everybody?'

'That sounds like a pleasant idea,' I said.

'And you can tell me every detail of your adventure,' she added. 'I'm longing to hear it all. I hope it's full of dungeons and secret passages and skeletons.'

'Not quite but near enough.'

'And romantic encounters?'

'Don't be silly!' I said, but warmed at the thought.

Sophie acquired a small basket from the kitchen and, finding that food had already been set out on the dining room, she went there for our picnic supplies. Meanwhile I had found a couple of cushions and a rug.

'Lady Denby is fulminating all over the place,' Sophie reported. 'She's complaining about Colonel Hartley giving everyone orders and taking over the house by organizing the search. Papa said if he didn't do it no one else would unless Lady Denby fancied herself as Boadicea. She didn't like that. Then she asked why *he* wasn't helping and he said he would after he'd had something to eat.'

'That is typical of your father, Sophie. I don't think he's lacking in courage or enterprise but the comforts of life come first.'

'I said Colonel Hartley hadn't eaten anything but Papa said he was used to it and probably didn't notice.'

'Who else was there?'

'Sir Ralph's had a tray taken to his room as he's having a lie-down. Elinor's in the dining room with Papa and Lady Denby. Rowland's back and I think his mother wanted him to stay with her but he's helping with the search, which is a point in his favour. The Lawrences are there but don't seem very happy. They must be wondering what sort of madhouse this is.'

'I think the Colonel would have preferred us to stay with the others.'

'Well, I couldn't stand any more of her ladyship at present. She really is unbearable at times.'

'Elinor and young Frederick Lawrence seem to have taken to each other.'

'Oh yes, they're sitting side by side, deep in conversation. He's decidedly plain but then, so is she. I'm hoping I can persuade her to do something with her hair and wear more attractive clothes.'

'He isn't so *very* plain. He has nice thick dark hair and a decent figure.'

'I'm sure he's pleasant enough but he seems rather dull. Elinor doesn't seem to mind but then, they share an interest in music. . . .'

We chatted on lightly until we came upon Sam Bates on the top landing.

'Where are you two ladies off to, if I may be so bold as to ask?' he enquired.

'We're going to have a picnic on the roof, away from everybody,' Sophie told him.

He looked doubtful. 'I suppose that's all right. I think Colonel Hartley would rather you didn't venture anywhere on your own, but we've already been up there. Not a sign of him.'

We went on our way and came to the little twisting stair that led to the door onto the roof. I led the way, Sophie close behind, and I shifted the cushions under my left arm whilst I opened the door. Even as I stepped across the threshold I knew something was wrong and I froze. I could see the toe of a glossy Hessian boot protruding at the base of one the chimneys.

'Go back, Sophie!' I hissed. 'He's here, go back!'

I heard her moving away behind me and I hoped to follow her but it was too late. Frank Lawrence stepped out into full view, a pistol in his hand.

# CHAPTER TWENTY-SIX

He looked startled to see me but soon recovered his composure.

'So you got out? I knew someone had raised the hue and cry but I didn't think it could be you. Don't attempt to retreat or I'll be compelled to shoot you. Move away from the door.'

I did as he said, still foolishly hugging the cushions and rug. If only I could keep him talking until help arrived! I had only to wait for Sophie to report what had happened – but the time that might take was incalculable with people scattered all over the house.

'You really are the most tiresome woman!' he declared. 'I think I may have to shoot you after all to secure your silence but there's the problem of your disposal.'

'Won't shooting me make a lot of noise and bring people running?'

'It would take them a few minutes to get up here and by then I'd have got away.'

'Sam Bates said they'd already searched the roof.'

'Bates? Oh, that devoted slave of 'Armless 'Artley. Used to be a sergeant or something, I believe, when they were playing at soldiers. No, I hid in one of the attics and managed to slip up here after the search was made.'

'Very clever of you!'

'Pity I didn't escape earlier but there were too many people about.'

'But you can't possibly get away with yet another crime – there's too much evidence against you.'

'Well, it's certainly not turned out as I planned, but if I can get down to Devonshire fast I may well be able to seize at least some of the fortune due to me and cross over to France, change my name again, and lose myself – a rich Englishman touring the Continent. Not the life I'd intended to lead but a good second-best.'

'But how did you persuade Louisa Thorpe to bring you here? How did you meet her?'

'By accident at first. I was tracking down James Rushworth. I found he'd been working as a clerk in the City. Then he answered an advertisement for a tutor from a factory owner in Manchester. He travelled up there on the stage and had the bulk of his luggage sent on later by his landlady. She knew his address.

'When I got to Manchester I entered into the social life of the town – concerts, assemblies, plays and the like. Mrs Thorpe was quite an ornament to society in those parts. She made a dead set at me and I must say at that point I found her decidedly attractive, especially when she told me she had a dear friend who had moved into Lovegrove Priory.

'Now, Rushworth had left his tutor's job a year before but they knew where he'd gone. The first part of the problem was solved – I knew where Rushworth was living and if I played my cards right I'd have the means of getting myself invited here. We'd never met so there was no possibility of his recognizing me.

'It took a little time, of course, but that was no problem; I had to wait until Louisa was invited to Lovegrove but by that time she couldn't do without me so I came along in the guise of her nephew.'

'Who is at present eating cold chicken downstairs.'

He obviously had no idea that Sophie had come up with me and for that I was profoundly thankful.

'Now you can answer some questions for me. How did you enjoy your sojourn in the dark with the mutilated Colonel? I trust he was a perfect gentleman?'

'He could scarcely be anything else as he *is* one. Anyway, we weren't in the dark – we'd got your tinderbox and a candle.'

'The devil you had!'

'And we found the hidden door and got down into the tunnel and then up into the priory ruins.'

'Bravo! – or should it be "bravi" as there are two of you? That makes me think I might go to Italy – plenty of sun and wine and beautiful women. Now I really think we have talked enough and the time has come to say good-bye . . .'

At that moment a shot rang out from the doorway, followed by the acrid smell of gunsmoke. Frank staggered against a chimney and dropped his pistol.

'You should have let me shoot him, sir, I'm a better shot than you,' I heard Sam Bates's voice.

'I only wanted to wing him – grab hold of him and I'll get his pistol.'

Bates ran forward and seized Frank by both arms, twisting them behind him. This obviously caused considerable pain, as he could not restrain a yelp, but Bates seemed to be enjoying himself.

'This is nothing compared to what Colonel Hartley has been through. I'd like to see your arm smashed to a bloody pulp and the surgeon take nearly twenty minutes to cut it off and he not uttering so much as a groan. What you've got is a scratch.'

'Is this really necessary?'

Bates ignored him. 'I need something to tie his hands, sir.'

The Colonel started to loosen his neckcloth but I pulled off my sash and ran over to Bates. What happened next was so quick and unexpected that even when I tried to recall it afterward I could scarcely decide exactly what had happened.

I do know that Frank Lawrence kicked me violently on the shin so that I was nearly thrown off my feet. Bates flung out an arm to steady me and Frank, free from his grip, pulled out a pocket pistol and aimed it at me.

'Now stand back or I'll shoot Miss Tyler. Stand over there,' he ordered and jerked his head towards a place near the door. A pocket pistol is not particularly accurate at a distance so I suppose that is why he wanted to keep me near.

I found myself standing close to where I had dropped the cushions. He backed towards the door and felt with his foot for the step. I ducked quickly and threw one of the cushions at his raised foot. He slipped, the pistol went off harmlessly and he fell backwards down the stairs. Bates soon leapt on him and hauled him up again. Now I could see that there was blood pouring down Frank's hand from the wound on his right shoulder. He cast a despairing look at me, kicked wildly out at Bates, ran headlong for the parapet and leapt over.

We all ran to the battlemented wall and looked down. Frank's twisted body lay on the stone-flagged terrace below.

'I hoped he'd hang,' muttered Bates.

'Yes,' said the Colonel, 'but this will save everyone a great deal of trouble.'

I stared at that crumpled body; it looked so small and unreal. One so full of life, however evil, ought not to end his days like that, though I suppose it was better than the fate envisaged by Sam Bates. I turned away, suddenly weak and trembling. The two men viewed the remains in a calm and curiously detached way. It's their profession, I thought.

'Charlotte!' I heard the Colonel's voice. 'He kicked you – are you much hurt? Let me see – oh, forget modesty – it may need attention. I've seen your legs before, don't forget.'

I thought Sam Bates looked rather surprised. Then I raised my skirt and revealed my torn stocking and a nasty bleeding contusion underneath.

'He's put his mark on both of us,' he said. 'You'd better get this washed and bandaged. Thank God you're safe. That was a very foolish thing to do – he could have shot you.'

'But brave and quick-thinking, sir.' Bates interposed. 'We could have done with this young lady in the regiment.'

'Did it really take twenty minutes to amputate your arm?'

'Oh, that – I had the misfortune to be wounded at the end of the battle rather than the beginning so the instruments were blunt. I must admit I wasn't quite as heroic as Bates claimed. Towards the end I swore at the surgeon, but he didn't seem to mind.'

At that moment we heard voices behind us and George

appeared with two of the menservants and Sophie close behind. She ran to me and hugged me in a tearful embrace.

'Oh – what have you been doing?' she cried. 'What a dreadful day! I think you've been trying to get yourself killed. I was sure he was going to shoot you. I ran down and found Colonel Hartley and he told me to go to Papa. I was so worried!'

George embraced me affectionately. 'Really, Char, I don't know what we're going to do with you. I always thought Sophie would be the one to get into mischief.'

Sophie attempted to look over the parapet but was prevented from doing so by Colonel Hartley.

'What are you going to do with him – put him in the laundry?' she enquired.

'I expect so but I don't see any reason for you to be involved. I understand you planned to go home tomorrow?'

'We hoped so,' said George ruefully, 'but I suppose we'll have to postpone our departure yet again.'

'It's not strictly necessary. There are two perfectly adequate witnesses in Bates and me and I'm sure that now the murderer is dead, the coroner will be quite content to keep the proceedings quiet in order to spare the Denby family further trouble. If you make a written statement I'm sure that will suffice,' he told me.

George looked relieved. 'We'll all be glad to get away,' he said.

'I'm sure you will.' Colonel Hartley gave me a despondent look and I was not quite sure what to make of it; regret perhaps, even yearning. His face still bore the grime of the morning's adventure and his scarred and swollen cheek distorted his expression.

We left the next morning at the same time as the Lawrences. Lady Denby and Sir Ralph saw us off with many regretful farewells. The former declared she was not at all sure she could go on living at Lovegrove after the succession of tragedies that had befallen the house.

'So if you come to stay with us again it may well be in another place. But we must keep in touch. I will let you know what transpires.'

When we were under way, Sophie said, anxiously, 'Do we have to invite them to stay with us in return? Sir Ralph would be an agreeable guest but—'

'Her ladyship is insufferable,' Elinor completed the sentence for her.

'Well, there's no need to think about it yet,' said George comfortably, glad to be returning to the peace and ease of Fairfield.

We passed the gates of the Hartleys' park a little while after leaving Lovegrove. I thought somehow he would be waiting there to say goodbye, but there was no one. I could have echoed Amelia Denby's cry the night Louisa Thorpe died: 'I feel so desolate!'

# CHAPTER TWENTY-SEVEN

George and Sophie settled back happily into our normal life at Fairfield. Elinor too seemed very pleased with her new surroundings and became quite cheerful and amiable.

'I asked her about Frederick Lawrence and she said she liked him but didn't really know him,' Sophie told me. 'I think she was encouraged by the fact that a young man showed a genuine interest in her. I've persuaded her to do something different with her hair and I've given her a couple of my sashes and lots of ribbons to brighten up her bonnets and gowns.'

'We'll make a flirt of her yet,' I smiled.

Colonel Hartley wrote to George twice giving details of the legal proceedings following the death of Frank Rushworth. Each letter concluded with kindest regards 'to your sister and daughter'.

Then there came a letter for me, written in his rapid, sloping hand. It consisted of little more than a couple of sentences:

'I think of you constantly; I hope you sometimes think of me. Let me know if you wish to see me again. Be assured I always have your best interests at heart. John Hartley.'

That was all. After our hazardous adventures, our closeness, that kiss . . . I wrote back, maintaining a rather reserved tone, saying that I certainly could not forget him and would be pleased to see him any time he was in the vicinity of Fairfield.

Several more weeks passed by. We heard from Lady Denby, who, having got over her resolution to leave Lovegrove, had begun to feel more secure. She was finishing her novel and was on good terms with Rowland, who had eventually settled in a cottage in Ashdale with his wife and child. I fancied that Carrie would not like a dull provincial life and would be pining for London but at least the baby, Arabella, had been introduced to her grandmama and Rowland was probably hoping his wife would soon be welcomed at Lovegrove.

There had been an inquest on Frank Rushworth and his crimes exposed. As expected a verdict of suicide was returned and the previous findings on his victims revised. This meant that the body of James Rushworth could at last be given Christian burial.

The funeral took place at Lovegrove parish church and was attended by the dead man's cousin who was next heir to the Devonshire estate. Colonel Hartley was also one of the chief mourners and although the congregation was small, the ceremony proceeded with appropriate dignity. Unfortunately the aged vicar, poor Mr Phillips, collapsed with a stroke after the service and was quite incapacitated. He was retiring from his duties and it was likely that young Frederick Lawrence would take over the living. I was pleased to hear this for Elinor's sake. Whatever came of their burgeoning friendship at least she would have a kindred spirit close at hand to share her interests.

The last part of Lady Denby's letter was most interesting for me: 'Colonel Hartley talks of visiting your part of the country soon. I am going to ask him to call on you and escort Elinor home. Her father misses her.'

The following week took us into September and already a misty melancholy had settled over the early mornings – a hint of the coming autumn. One golden afternoon I was sitting on the terrace with the two girls. I was sketching, Sophie sewing and Elinor reading.

Sophie looked up suddenly. 'Here's Papa!' she said.

George came towards us smiling and held out his hands to me. 'Someone is here to see you,' he said. 'He says he'd prefer to meet you outside. Go round to the front of the house.' He leaned closer and kissed me on the cheek.

'I think I know what all this is about,' he whispered. 'I wish you every happiness.'

There was no need to ask who the visitor might be. I ran around the house and then slowed to a decorous walk, not wishing to appear too eager. He stood between the columns of the porch, a tall, broad-shouldered figure in a dark-blue coat with an empty sleeve.

'Colonel Hartley,' I said, extending my hand. 'I am so glad to see you.'

'I can't call you Miss Tyler – not now – and I thought I once asked you to call me John.'

'So you did, but in very unusual circumstances. It seems a long time ago now and not quite real.'

'Shall we walk? Out of sight of the house. Take my arm – it will always have to be the right one.'

'I wondered why you never came to say goodbye when we left Lovegrove.'

'It was not because I didn't want to but I thought it best to put an interval between us. We had known each other only a short time but we had grown very close. Shared danger draws people together but there's not necessarily any real depth to it – nothing permanent. I wanted you to be absolutely sure of your feelings. Back in your old home you could have looked on me very differently.'

'Oh, no!'

'I didn't want you to imagine you loved me because we once clung together for comfort and kissed from sheer joy and relief at having survived. I wanted to give you a chance to break free without feeling any obligation.'

'I've missed you more than I can say,' I said. We were surrounded by trees, rustling in the breeze, screening us from the rest of the world.

He drew me close and we exchanged a long and increasingly passionate kiss.

'I've been wanting to do that since the day we met,' he said at last, 'but at that stage I had to show restraint. Besides . . .' He hesitated a little. 'I'm such a disfigured, carved-up wreck I feared I might repulse you.'

In reply I stood on tiptoe and kissed the furrow in his cheek.

'Ah,' he smiled, 'that's encouraging! I have several other scars which you can't see at present but I hope it won't be too long before you make their acquaintance.'

'Very soon, I hope.'

'I think we'd better marry as early as legally possible before you change your mind and run off with some handsome young rake.'

'How could I?'

'At least he'd have two arms to embrace you.'

'One is quite enough. I'm sure Lady Hamilton had no complaints.'

We kissed again and were married by licence before the month was out.